THE DRAGON AT THE EDGE OF THE MAP

P. A. WILSON

FREE EBOOK

Claim your copy of Buying Into Death when you sign up for my newsletter and follow Charity as she solves her fastest case yet!

1

———

onique climbed the last set of stairs to her fifth floor apartment. She made herself a promise to get in better shape. She shouldn't be out of breath, even with the smoking. It was a week until her birthday, another year gone. This birthday was a milestone, for her, not for most people. Thirty-six, half her life lived before what her father had done, and half her life after. If you could call what she did living, perhaps it was just surviving.

The gig tonight had been great. The glow of appreciation from the audience still warmed her. It was two am, but maybe Rafe would still be awake, maybe the night didn't have to end. Maybe the void would be filled for a little while longer.

Sorting her apartment key to the top of the ring, she pushed open the stairwell door. The sight at the end of the hall, across from her own apartment, stopped her from taking the next step. Two men in overcoats and cheap suits stood staring through the open door of her neighbor's apartment. The stairwell door slammed behind her, and both men turned to stare.

Police. She reached behind her for the door, not sure why she felt the need to flee, but already thinking of where she'd go.

A uniformed cop stepped out of the apartment and whispered something to one of the men. The other took a step toward her. He held out his ID and she saw a shield on the card, one she didn't recognize. It didn't matter, they were obviously cops; she'd learned to recognize the attitude.

"Ma'am, this floor is closed."

Monique shook her head and stepped forward. No one was going to tell her she couldn't get into her home. She needed a shower, and a meal. "I live there," she said, pointing to her door. "What's going on?"

The detective – he must be a detective that kind of suit was almost a uniform for them – made a comment to his partner. Monique couldn't make out the words, but she figured it was something to do with making her go away. He turned back and said, "If you would like to answer a few questions, we can let you into your apartment."

He looked reasonable, and Monique didn't have anything to hide. She shoved away a little voice that told her to call a lawyer before talking to them, that the last time she'd talked to a detective it hadn't turned out well. "Sure, let's get this over with."

She tried not to look through the open door as she passed. She hated the kind of people who slowed down to look at accidents. She told herself that whatever was in there wouldn't be good. But her head turned almost as though someone had moved it for her. The uniformed cop pulled the door shut, but it was too late. She'd seen.

There was a lot of blood and a body. He, or maybe it, now that he was dead, was broken apart like someone had taken an ax and chopped him into two pieces at the waist.

Monique closed her eyes and slipped her key into the lock, feeling the presence of the cops behind her, reassuring now instead of threatening. She glanced at the mirror in the hall, needing to know what the cops were seeing. Her normally pale skin looked dull, reflecting the shock she felt from the scene across the hall, her green eyes shining from behind her messy bangs.

The shaking was already starting. She clenched her fist to keep the panic from taking over. It stopped the trembling but didn't wipe out the vision of all the blood. She could handle this. She'd handled worse. She had to keep it together. Swallowing the bile percolating in the back of her throat, Monique pointed to the stools at the kitchen counter and turned on the coffee pot. She held up two mugs in query, and both detectives nodded. "Okay, what do you want to ask?"

"Thanks," the first detective said. "I'm Detective Watson, Larry. This is my partner, Mike Adams." The other cop, younger than Watson, nodded. "Let's start with your name?"

She cleared her throat, hoping they didn't take it as a sign of weakness. "Monique Duchesne." She knew better than to volunteer any information. Anything she offered would be used as a thread to find questions that she wouldn't want to answer.

"And how long have you lived here?"

She noticed Adams write in the notebook while Watson asked the questions. "Five years." The coffee started dripping, so she went to get the milk from the fridge.

"Where do you come from?"

That was an odd question. "What do you mean?"

"You know, we all came here from somewhere. Where did your folks come from?"

"Why?"

Watson shrugged. "Just curious. Why don't you want to answer?"

There it was. Cops didn't like it when you held back information. Even if the question had nothing to do with whatever crime they were investigating. Monique was tempted to tell him to mind his own business, but she worried that he'd use that against her. "My dad emigrated from Yugoslavia. My mom was fourth generation Canadian."

He nodded, and Adams made a note. Watson continued. "And what do you do, Monique? For a living?"

Damn. The questions were going to come no matter what she did. "I sing at Blue Scene and I do a bit of tour guide stuff. Why do you need to know that?"

Mike Adams looked up from his notebook. "I thought I recognized you. You've got a great voice."

Monique smiled, but didn't let down her guard as she poured coffee. "Thanks. So why do you need to know about my work?"

Detective Watson ignored her question and sipped his coffee. "So is that where you were tonight?"

"Yes, I got there around nine and left about fifteen minutes before you saw me. Is this where I should tell you I want my lawyer?"

"No, the victim's been dead more than an hour. We got an anonymous call and when we got here... well, you saw what we saw. I'm sorry about that." He rubbed his forehead and Monique realized she wasn't the only one pretending to be unaffected by the horror across the hall.

Another sip and Watson asked, "Did you know him?"

She loosened her grip on the mug before she snapped the handle. The panic wouldn't push away, this needed to be over soon, or she'd collapse while they were in her home. She shook her head and rubbed at a spot on the counter. "He only moved in last month. I said hi to him once, and I think he had an accent, maybe eastern European. It was hard to tell from just a 'good morning'. The guy liked Death Metal and didn't under-stand you could play music at less than full volume."

"Did he have any visitors?" Watson was watching her closely.

Monique shook her head again and rose to put her mug in

the sink. Leaning against the counter, she said, "I didn't pay much attention. I don't remember hearing anyone knock on his door." She crossed her arms, hoping they would get the hint that she wanted to be finished with the questions.

The detectives rose leaving their half-empty coffee mugs on the table. "Thanks. I guess if there's anything else we need, we can reach you here?"

"Here or the club. Should I be worried about someone breaking in?"

Detective Adams slid his notebook into his pocket, retrieving a business card. "Make sure you lock your door, and don't open it to strangers. If you need anything, or something happens, call."

Monique took the card; a list of contact numbers filled the back. "So, it wasn't random?"

Detective Watson looked her up and down. Monique felt the dismissal in his glance. "We don't discuss open cases with the public. Just be careful, and you should be okay."

She kept her eyes on the floor as she let the two detectives out. Locking the door and shoving a chair under the handle to block any forced entry didn't make her feel any safer. She slid to the floor and gave up fighting the inevitable. The darkness crawled over her as she curled into a ball, trembling with the memory of the room across the hall.

MONIQUE UNTANGLED herself from the sheets and stretched the last vestiges of sleep from her body. She could hear Rafe in the kitchen. Judging by the fingers of light pushing through the slats of the blinds, it was lunchtime. She stumbled to the bathroom to brush her teeth and try to deal with the mess sleep had made of her hair.

She'd called Rafe an hour after the cops left. He'd buzzed

her into the building and waited at the elevator. His warmth and strength driving the last of the fear from her.

Ten minutes after leaving Rafe's bed, she snuck into the kitchen to wrap her arms around him. He made her feel safe, at least until she remembered that safety was just a temporary feeling. Her neighbor had probably felt safe. Her mother had too.

She pulled a mug from the cupboard and poured herself coffee. Rafe hated her smoking in his apartment, so she'd have to wait for her other vice.

"Afternoon, babe. You hungry?"

She watched him flip a grilled cheese sandwich in the pan. His strong hands holding the spatula delicately. His dark skin was as different from her pallor as everything else about him was. He glowed with health, and he carried a comfortable amount of padding on his frame. She was thin enough to garner looks of concern from strangers.

"You know I am."

He flipped the sandwich onto a plate and reached for the bread to start another. "Are you ready to tell me what exactly happened last night?"

Monique shrugged. When she'd called Rafe, she'd told him there was trouble with a neighbor. Leaving out the details meant she didn't have to argue with him about how unsafe her building was.

"What makes you think there's anything else to tell?" Monique added a pile of potato chips from the bag on the counter to her plate.

"Nightmares. You were fighting something all night." His attention was focused on the contents of the pan. "You'll feel better if you tell me what happened." He glanced at her. "You know I hate that you live there, so I won't mention it again."

"I like that building, and I can afford the rent." She also liked her independence and knew Rafe wanted her to move into his place. Monique wasn't ready for that, maybe never would be. It was an old argument and she didn't want to have it again. "Sorry."

"I said I wouldn't talk about it and I won't. But unless you plan to work this out in your sleep, you need to tell someone how you feel." He muttered something else to the pan as he flipped his own sandwich.

"I don't need to –"

He slapped the spatula on the counter. "You do. You keep saying you don't need to talk about your feelings, but you're human and that means you feel something. It will turn you sour, Monique. If you don't deal with this, it will dry you up and kill you."

Monique felt the familiar tightening of her stomach at the memory of the last time she'd talked about her feelings. But she didn't want to lose sleep, so maybe Rafe was right, talking about it would make it go away faster. "Okay. Look my neighbor got murdered last night. I'm fine. I didn't even know him." Rafe didn't know what it took to talk to a psychologist. How they twisted everything you told them.

"Did you see what they did to him?" Rafe dropped his plate onto the table. "If you did, it would explain your nightmares."

"What do you mean, what they did to him?" There was no hope of getting out of this without a fight if Rafe had any of the details.

"I knew something happened. I checked the police radio transmissions. And then I called my friend in the morgue. He told me what the body looked like when it came in." Rafe had friends all over the city in all kinds of professions. His work as an investigative blogger meant he needed contacts. The goriest stories brought the most hits to his blog, and that meant more affiliate money. Monique didn't like the fact that he'd used those contacts on her. That he'd known what happened before she decided to tell him, like he was testing her.

No longer hungry, Monique pushed her plate away. Her hands reaching for the pack of cigarettes in her purse before remembering Rafe had no ashtrays. "Okay. Yes I did see it. Yes, it was horrible, but I am fine. I didn't know the guy. From what the cops said, it was personal, so I'm fine. I'm fine." She hated the shake in her voice at the end.

Rafe pushed her plate back toward her. "Eat before you get so thin you disappear. If you were okay, why did you call me? If you are okay, why did you have nightmares?"

"I called you because I didn't want to spend the night alone. I was already going to call you before I saw the… and I don't know why I had nightmares." She took a bite of the sandwich hoping she could get it down her tightening throat. At least it would give her some time to cool off before she ended up saying something that would hurt him. That's what always happened.

"You say that all the time. Nothing bothers you apparently."

Monique didn't want to have this argument, not now and, preferably, not ever. "I just don't see the point of talking about feeling crappy. I really don't feel that bad about it. Is that wrong? You used to like the fact that I didn't weep over stupid things." And it was safer not to care too much.

Rafe sighed, and she could see him work to hold in his temper. "Sometimes I feel like I'm the only one who feels anything in this relationship." He looked away from her. "If it's just about the sex, let me know."

"It's not." She stood and went to the living area of the open plan apartment. "I'm going home. I think it's best if we don't talk for a couple of days." If he really loved her, he'd let it go. Maybe a few days apart would cool everything down again. She started for the door.

"Are you going to call me? Or is this your way of ending it? I deserve better than this if it is." His voice was quiet, and Monique knew she'd hurt him more than she'd intended.

"I'll call you," she said as she left.

Waiting for the elevator, she wondered if he was right. Was this relationship all about the sex? Why did he have to want more than she could give? He knew why she couldn't give him more, and it had been enough until recently.

Perhaps it was time to end it, before he got hurt. Perhaps she should take advantage of this fight to leave.

When the elevator arrived, Monique pulled out her cigarettes, ready to light up as soon as she stepped out of the front door of his building. Nicotine helped fill that hole inside where other people probably kept the feelings she hadn't felt since her eighteenth birthday.

Later, Monique turned away from her window. Staring at the rain wasn't going to get her anywhere. If Rafe wanted to break up, so be it. She would survive. She always survived. She slipped her iPod into the speaker dock and let it run through her favorite playlist. Music always helped no matter what mood she was in or how bad the day had been. Nerves were making her jumpy. She needed to do something. The weak light through the window didn't show it, but her home needed a cleaning. Anything that would help take her mind off the memory of the blood across the hall.

It didn't take long, but the familiar steps of dusting, polishing, and scouring brought a measure of peace. The staleness that dulled her senses lifted, replaced with the clean sharp smell of lemon and bleach. Monique threw the cleaning cloths into the laundry basket then leaned out through the open window and lit a cigarette, inhaling deeply. The rain had stopped while she was cleaning, the clouds evaporating to reveal the sky, pale blue just waiting for the sun to set and display stars.

She knew logically that the argument with Rafe wasn't going to end the relationship. In her head, the reality of his accusation rang true, and she couldn't argue against anything he'd said. In her heart, something twisted the words into weapons and truth didn't matter. It wasn't her fault she couldn't feel anything. He knew her history, and he knew what she'd overcome. She hated that he was trying to change her. She knew she was broken. She didn't need anyone to fix her.

Broken had worked for the last eighteen years.

She shook her head and stubbed the cigarette into the ashtray she held. Thinking wouldn't solve the problem. She needed to talk to Rafe, but she also needed to take some time to get over the fight first. If she called him right now, there was a real chance she'd make things worse while trying to fix them.

In the kitchen, Monique started a pot of coffee and then picked up the material Walk in The Past had sent about the new ghost walk she was leading in a couple of days. Vancouver had enough history to make hundreds of different tours, and she filled some time with leading tourists through the more seedy parts of town. The stories she told about the history of the area seemed to entertain. Some of them were true, and some complete fiction.

Halfway through the material, Monique heard a door slam across the hall. Fear shot through her entire body. Were the police back? She walked to the peephole and glanced out, but there was nothing to see. Monique leaned against the door. The noise had definitely come from across the hall. Wanting to avoid going back to picking over her relationship defects, and bored with the reading material, she turned the lock quietly and darted across the hall.

Monique tried to look through the peephole into the apartment, but the distortion blurred all the details. She leaned against the door, careful not to break the crime tape, and listened. Yes, there was something going on in there. Someone was tossing heavy things around.

She pushed away from the door and ducked back into her own apartment. Should she call the police? What if it was something innocent? She reached for the phone to call Rafe for advice before she remembered the fight.

She put her eye to her own peephole, but there was no one in the hall. She knew that calling the cops was the right thing to do. She knew it wasn't something innocent. Why would someone innocently be going through the murdered guy's apartment? She glanced at the phone and made her decision.

"Hey, cut it out," a woman shrieked.

Monique ran back to the door to see who had come from the apartment. It wasn't a stranger. Mac, the guy who lived next door stood in her line of sight. He had his arm around a skinny blond chick, a bottle of Jack in the hand dangling near her breasts. He slobbered a kiss on her cheek and then elbowed his door open. They fell through it, both giggling.

Glancing at the apartment across from her, Monique decided to wait. If she called the cops now, she didn't have any details. If she kept watch, maybe she would see something useful. She hated her father for many things, but mostly right now, because he'd made her afraid of the police, and that was making her look for excuses to delay the call.

Monique took the phone from its cradle and held it ready to call if something happened.

Keeping her eye to the peephole, she couldn't help imagining what was going on in the apartment. Why would someone need to come back there? Had they used a key? She tried to think back over the month since the guy had moved in. Alexi, that was his name. She'd told the police she hadn't noticed any visitors, was that really the case? There was that one time, some older guy was banging on Alexi's door. But he wasn't home, so that probably doesn't count.

Music started thumping out of Mac's apartment. It sounded

like a porn soundtrack. Monique snorted a laugh. At least someone was having fun.

She checked the clock. Whoever was in the apartment had been there for fifteen minutes. They might not come out for a while. If she'd phoned the cops when she first heard the door, they would be here by now. She pressed 911 and waited for the response. Her hand trembled. She shook it out to release the tension, hoping that it would work, and that the trembling wasn't the start of a panic attack.

"911 what is your emergency?"

"I... um, I saw someone go into an apartment," she said. Damn nerves, damn history.

"Ma'am?"

Monique took a breath. "Sorry. I live across from the guy who got murdered... at the Montrose... on 15th... near Main. Someone is in the apartment."

"The police are on their way. Are you in danger?"

Keeping her eye on the door across the way, Monique said, "No. Whoever it is doesn't know I heard anything. They are still in there. I heard them tossing stuff around."

"The police will be there in two minutes. I'll stay on the line with you until they arrive."

"No, I'm fine. I'll wait for them. Thanks." Monique hung up the phone and put it back on the cradle.

A sound drew her back to the peephole. A man, tall, skinny, and bald was locking the door behind him. He turned to Mac's door and said something Monique couldn't make out, but he followed it with a dirty leer.

Then he turned to stare at her apartment.

She jumped back at the sight of his dark eyes burning through the door. He looked like something from a horror movie. The one monster that looked human until you got close and saw the blankness behind his eyes.

Telling herself he couldn't see her, Monique put her eye back to the peephole and was relieved that his gaze was on the floor. She watched him bend and retrieve a black gym bag from the carpet. He checked the weight of the bag and then headed to the stairwell.

The elevator chimed just as she heard the stairwell door bang shut. Monique pulled open her door to see detectives Watson and Adams step into the hall.

"He went down the stairs," she kept her voice quiet, not wanting the man to know she'd seen anything. "He just went down."

The two detectives ripped open the door and raced though. "Stop! Police!"

Monique heard the words then a clatter of feet on the uncarpeted stairs. Glancing at Mac's door in case the sound had penetrated the bump kachunk of the music, Monique retreated to her apartment. If the cops were successful, she was done for the day. That would be fine. She didn't need to get involved. She could get back to her life.

Monique grabbed a bottle of Malbec from the rack and unscrewed the top. After pouring a glass, she opened all the windows and lit a cigarette. To hell with the smell. Wine glass in hand, she stood inside the living room watching the street, hoping to see the arrest. Nothing but a few pedestrians and some guy trying to park a jeep in a space big enough for a Smart car.

She stubbed out the cigarette and blew the last lungful of smoke through the open window.

Maybe it happened out in the alley. She knew the cops didn't need to let her know what happened, but it would be nice. The memory of those black eyes burning through the peephole made her skin crawl. There was no way he would know she was there. It was just a coincidence.

She reached for her cellphone. Maybe calling Rafe would help her settle. As her fingers traced the pattern to unlock it, she decided to wait. Phoning Rafe only when she was struggling seemed unfair. If she wasn't ready to commit to him, she shouldn't be ready to use him.

In the kitchen, she topped off the wine and reached for a package of Ramen noodles. Then dropped them as someone banged on her door, and the shock stopped her heart. She braced herself on the counter to stop the sudden rush of dizziness that flooded her when her heart started again, pounding so hard it felt like she was jerking to a four-part beat.

"Hang on," she called, taking one last deep breath before she swallowed a gulp of wine.

"Ms. Duchesne?" It was Watson and he sounded worried.

If they were here, the guy must have gotten away. "Yes, just a second." She checked through the peephole before opening the door, just in case.

"Are you okay?" Detective Adams asked.

Monique recognized the canned emotions, meant to put a suspect, or victim, at ease. The good cop part of the equation. She knew to avoid believing he really cared. "I'm fine. He didn't see me. I swear I didn't confront him. Just tell me what happened. Is he still out there?"

"I can't tell you much," Watson said, glancing at the coffee pot.

Monique wasn't planning to make them feel at home, so she ignored his hint. "Does that mean you didn't catch him?"

Adams pulled out his notebook and waited for Watson to take the lead.

"We missed him. He could have hidden too many places when he went out the back. We need to know exactly what happened. Start with what you saw."

Taking a sip of her wine, Monique sat on one of the stools at the counter. "I heard a noise.... the door slamming across the hall. I wasn't sure what was going on, so I listened at the door and heard someone banging around inside."

Watson leaned against the counter and crossed his arms. "Why didn't you call us then?"

"How do you know I didn't?"

"Did you? Was he only in there a minute or two?"

Monique couldn't think of a way to avoid the question, so she shrugged. "I wasn't sure that there was any problem. It could have been you guys. I would have looked pretty stupid calling the cops if it was you."

He twisted his lips then relaxed as though he'd made a decision. "No you wouldn't. What you did was stupid. If it happens again, call. So you want to give your statement here, in your apartment?"

Wary of the change in his attitude, Monique said, "Here is fine. Like I said, I heard someone banging around the apartment. Then I decided to call. I don't know maybe I realized cops would have removed the crime tape, or something."

Adams was scribbling notes. "What did you see?"

"When I was on the phone the guy came out. Maybe fifty, around six foot, maybe a couple of hundred pounds... No, he was really thin, probably more like one-eighty. Shaved head, gray stubble. Am I going too fast?"

Adams looked up. "No, carry on."

"Okay. Weird eyes. Black like they were all pupil. Oh, maybe he was high."

"Any distinguishing marks? Scars? Tattoos?"

Monique closed her eyes and reluctantly drew on the memory of that face. "No. Just the eyes were weird."

"Anything else?"

She ran the memory like a movie. "He had a black gym bag.

It seemed heavy, but there was no sound when he lifted it, so whatever was inside it wasn't hard, or metal."

Watson straightened. "Have you ever seen him before?"

Monique shook her head. Then memory flashed. "Wait. There was a tattoo on his hand, the back of his hand. It was faded but I think it was an eagle... it was clutching something square." She held out her hand for the notebook. "Let me draw it for you." She sketched quickly. An eagle's head in profile, but she couldn't put any detail around the square. She pushed it back to Adams.

"Anything else?" Watson asked.

"No that's it. So, you can go now." The words felt harsh, but Monique wanted them out of her house, wanted to start putting this behind her. She'd had plenty of practice at that.

"Do you have somewhere else to stay?" Watson actually looked like he cared. She reminded herself he was just playing good cop.

"I'm fine here." Monique hoped she was right, but what if the guy came back? "He doesn't know I called you." If he came looking, there were only six apartments on the floor. It wouldn't take him long to figure out who did call. "It could have been someone downstairs, or anyone who saw him come into the building. Anyway, what are you going to do?"

"We'll send a team to check out the apartment. They'll remove the tape like you thought, so you don't think there's a problem. Then we'll get back to the investigation." Watson gestured to Adams. "We have to go. Be careful, Ms. Duchesne."

Monique strode to the door and pulled it open. "I'm a big girl. I won't open my door to strangers. Just catch the guy, and we'll all be fine."

"It's on the list of cases. We'll solve it, just be careful."

She watched them check the lock on the door across the hall and then leave. When the elevator closed, Monique stepped back into her apartment and locked herself in. Pulling a chair away from the dining table, she jammed it under the handle again.

What did he mean? It's on the list of cases? How many of these kinds of brutal murders did they have on the list? What did it take for a case to get priority?

How long did she need to keep the door locked?

3

Monique curled up on the couch, trying to put the events of the last hour into the past. Shoving the memory into the same place that she put everything she didn't want to deal with. It worked in the past. It would work now.

She stretched out and wrapped the chenille throw around her shoulders. Closing her eyes, she imagined a peaceful time. She realized that was only yesterday, right after her gig. She'd been looking forward to a late night tryst and a full day's sleep. What she'd gotten was a fight with Rafe and a brutal intrusion into her well-controlled life.

Her imagination couldn't overcome the vision of blood all over the floor next door and satanic eyes of that intruder. She struggled to unwrap herself and then put the wine bottle on the coffee table next to her. She swallowed her half-full glass and then refilled it. The alcohol would help her sleep, and after a good sleep, she would be ready to get back to normal. She took another gulp of wine and lay back on the couch. It was getting dark. Maybe she should call Rafe. Maybe it would be better to spend a few days at his place. Swallow her fears, and let him talk to her about trust, and emotions, and all the things she kept running from.

The phone rang, tearing her out of a doze. It was full dark outside, and the room was cold. Monique ran for the phone with the throw around her shoulders. "Rafe?" She hoped.

"No, sis," her brother said.

She let the hope drop away. "Didi, what do you want?" He usually wanted money to feed his habit.

"You always think I want something, Nique."

"You always want something. Spit it out, Didi, I've had a bad day." She closed the window.

"I think you'll be happy, Nique. I'm going into rehab."

Monique rubbed the bridge of her nose. If he meant it, she was happy he'd gotten this far; to be ready to kick the habit. Heroin was all around her. It was the bane of the jazz world. She'd never been tempted, but her brother had run to it as though it was a safe haven. Everyone handled life's shit differently. Who was saying her way was better? "Where are you going?"

"Life Clinic. They said I could come tomorrow." His voice was shaky. "Can I leave some of my stuff with you?"

"What kind of stuff?"

"Jeez, Nique, nothing bad," Didi said, a whine creeping into his voice. "It's just a couple of bags."

She really wanted to believe he was turning his life around. But it wasn't the first time she'd fallen for his promise to get clean. Could she trust him not to drop his stash with her? If he left something illegal, would Watson or Adams have any reason to find it? "Why can't you leave it at your place?"

There was no answer and Monique thought Didi had hung up. Then he finally said. "I don't have a place anymore. I got evicted. I'll find a new place when I get done with rehab. I promise, Nique. This time I'm getting straight."

Questions and arguments played out in her head. What was he going to do tonight for a bed? Why couldn't the clinic take him tonight, isn't that what happened? "What's different this time, Didi? I want to help, I do, but we've been through this before."

"I've hit the bottom this time. I never thought I'd get this low, Nique. I… look never mind what I did, I just don't want it to get any worse. Please, Nique."

"Okay, Didi. Come over, stay the night. I'll take you to rehab in the morning." She let herself hope it would be the last time he needed to detox.

"Thanks, Nique. Hey, can we have pizza? And watch a movie? Like when we were kids?"

"Sure, how long before you get here?"

Didi ended the call. Frustrated, Monique started to dig through a pile of old DVDs. They'd call for food when Didi arrived.

A knock at the door startled her. She hated the way her life was starting to run on fear. She crept to the peephole and saw Didi standing in the hall. He listed to the left and his face was covered with bruises, but his grin was the same as when he was five years old and realized for the first time that he could charm his way out of any scrape.

Monique took the chair away and pulled open the door. "You are going to tell me what happened as soon as I get some food into you."

He picked up his stuff, two plastic grocery bags bulging with clothes. "You look like you haven't eaten in six months, Nique. You make me look robust." He kissed her cheek and dropped the bags into the corner of the dining area.

Monique watched him limp across to the couch. It looked like whoever had administered the beating knew exactly how much damage to do without killing Didi. She called for a large pizza and a liter of Coke before joining him. "What happened?"

"I thought I was going to get fed before I had to tell."

"Don't mess with me, Didi. I've seen enough crap today. Tell me."

He shifted on the couch and grimaced. "I got in debt with the wrong people. They persuaded me to make an effort to repay." He touched the wine bottle. "Any chance of a glass for medicinal purposes?"

Booze had never been Didi's problem, so Monique retrieved a glass from the kitchen. "This is the last of it. How much do you owe these people?" She had some savings. If Didi needed it, he could have it all. One day she wouldn't be able to help him, but that was one day.

"Nothing." He sipped the wine. "Nice drink, Nique."

"How did you pay them back?"

He glanced away, at the television, at the movies spread out on the floor beside the television, anywhere but at her.

"Didi, how did you pay them?"

"That's the thing. Nique, don't be mad. I had to turn some tricks for them." He swallowed the entire glass of wine. "That's what convinced me to check into rehab. I've done some shitty things. I know I've been an embarrassment, but I've never turned tricks. And I never want to do that again."

Monique tried not to react. Sometimes he just seemed determined to make the worse choice. "I wish you had come to me. I could have –"

He held up a hand. "No, Nique. It's past. I don't want to think about what I should have done."

"Fine." Monique regretted the tone as soon as the word was out. "Sorry, I guess I'm taking my night out on you."

Didi shrugged. "What happened? Bad set at the club?"

"The cops were here – twice."

Didi jerked a look at the door as if the police would barge in. "Why?"

"There was a murder."

"Shit, Nique. Did they think you did it?"

Monique shook her head. "No. But it brought back memories."

"Yeah, those memories aren't ever too far away." He tossed back the last drops of his wine. "If they come after you the way they did before..."

"They won't." She crossed her fingers that she wasn't tempting fate.

"Do you know who got killed?"

"The guy across the hall. I didn't know him. Some Eastern European guy."

Didi glanced at her door again. "I know some of those guys."

"How do you know people like that?"

Didi laughed. "I'm a junkie, Nique. I know all kinds of criminals. Plus, I got interested because of dad."

"Don't mention him."

"Yeah, I know. But you remember he told us he changed his name, right? When he came to Canada. Duchesne is French. He figured it would be better."

Monique swallowed her first reaction. She hated talking about her father, but Didi remembered the good times. That's because he hadn't been the first one home on that day.

Didi didn't need her to fight with him. He needed her support. "Yes, I remember, now let's not talk about that any longer. Tomorrow I'll take you to rehab. And I'll pick you up when it's done."

An image of Didi floated into her mind. He was lying in that pool of blood. If he was getting involved with the kind of people who could do that, he was in more trouble than she feared.

4

I t took hours to check Didi into the clinic. Monique refused to just drop him off and leave. By the time they finished, and she drove all the way back to Vancouver, and the club, there was barely time to warm up. She started working through her voice exercises, thinking, as usual, that she should quit smoking so she could save some time on this.

"Sounding a bit tight there, kid." Tess handed Monique a glass of water, warm and flavored with honey.

Monique swallowed the drink slowly, letting it soothe her throat. "Yeah, life's been a big pile of crap. Didi finally got to rock bottom. Some guy got murdered across from me. I had to deal with the cops." *Shittier for Didi and Alexi.*

"Sounds like you might need the night off. If you do, decide now so I can get someone to fill in. Julie isn't as good as you, but she's usually up for an extra gig." As far as Tess was concerned, the club came first. She owned it, and managed half the acts that performed there.

Monique shook her head. She needed the money from the gig and, more importantly, when she sang all the crap in her life faded away. "I'm good. I thought we'd start with a bit of pop jazz, warm up the audience. Loosen up the guys."

Tess laughed. Monique heard a touch of acid in the sound. "Sure, sugar. Just make sure they love you. It sells drinks when they do."

Nodding, Monique went back to her vocal exercises. Tess patted Monique's arm and then wandered out to the club. No doubt to harass some busboy about a poorly placed candle.

While she ran through scales, Monique couldn't put aside the thought that she had diminished Alexi's death with her comment. Telling herself that the police would take care of the investigation, and that would get him justice, didn't dampen the acid building in her stomach. She couldn't let that get in the way. She needed to relax, or it would come out in the songs. Heartbreak would be fine; it could make a listener cry. But guilt just soured the notes. Guilt about a stranger was a stupid way to ruin an evening, and she didn't feel guilt. She didn't feel anything for anyone. Didi's face flashed into her mind. She snapped her fingers to clear the thoughts and focused on the exercises.

Twenty minutes later, Ray, the piano player, looked into the room. "Are you done warming up? We need to get back in here. You know Tess doesn't want any of us out in the club when the room starts to fill."

Monique checked her watch before slipping it into her pocket – shiny things caught the stage lights – ten minutes until they were officially supposed to play the first note. That meant they had at least twenty minutes until Tess ordered them on stage. A little impatience meant a few more rounds at the bar. Tess may not be the warmest person Monique knew, but she knew how to make a buck.

"It's a good night for some sad songs, Monique," Ali said as he poured a shot of whiskey into his coffee mug. "How about we start with *Cry Me a River*?"

"You love the tear jerking songs, Ali," she said. "Maybe we should end with that – send them home to a good cry?"

Ali played the double bass in the combo. The sax player, Wes, completed the trio with Ray. They had all been playing jazz almost as long as Monique had been alive.

Ali narrowed his eyes. "You look like you need to sing something more like *It's a Wonderful World*. What's got you down?"

Did she want to tell them? Maybe it would get this shit out of her head. "Didi checked into rehab today." They didn't need to hear about the rest of it. It felt like this part of her life could be safe from death and blood.

Wes rubbed his arm. Monique knew that he struggled with his own addiction, checking in to rehab every couple of years only to fall off the wagon eventually. "It's hard, Monique. When you try to stop chasing the dragon, it comes looking for you. It helps to know someone believes you can do it."

"I know, Wes. I hope he can. I really do. It's just that I don't think he will."

Monique could see the memory of his last detox flash across his face as Wes looked away. "It's going to be bad tonight. He'll probably be feeling the beginning of the sweats and depression. It gets easier. No, that's not right. Not easier, but less violent."

The thought of Didi curled up on a hospital bed, tightened Monique's heart. "What can I do? How can I help him stay sober when it's done?"

Ray patted her arm. "You can't do anything. This is between Didi and the dragon. Believe me I've learned that the hard way." He wrapped his arm around Wes. "Haven't I, babe?"

"When I said we should start with a sad song, I meant a song, not real life. You three are bringing me down." Ali offered the whiskey bottle around. "I get the idea that Didi isn't your only problem, Monique. I mean you look like you been strung on a line and left in the rain. You have a fight with Rafe?"

Monique sighed. "Yeah, but that's just the usual. We'll be fine in a couple of days, or we won't. I can deal with that." Realizing she couldn't separate her two worlds, she told them about the murder. "I think the cops are going to back burner his case. They seemed happy to leave his apartment empty until I called about the break in. And I'm worried that Didi might be involved somehow." She saw the surprise on their faces. "No, not that he would be the killer. Oh God, no. I think maybe he gets his drugs from these people."

Tess strode into the room. "Five minutes. I hope you paid for that bottle, Ali."

He held up a hand. "Of course, Tess, I wouldn't want you to lose the profit. We'll be out on time, don't worry."

She clicked her tongue in disgust. "Be sure you are." Then she spun and left them.

Wes watched Tess leave and then turned to Monique. "If he's buying drugs from them, and that's all, he should be okay. Do you think he's selling?"

"I hope not."

"If he is using, they won't let him into the organization," Wes said.

Monique stretched her arms over her head and filled her lungs. Talking with the guys had lifted some of the weight of the last day. "I'll keep good thoughts. Okay, no more depressing talk. Let's do that set we were practicing last week, you know, the kind of creepy obsessive songs."

"Sounds good," Wes said. "I'm going out for a smoke, anyone else coming?"

All three men went to the alley to indulge. Monique never smoked before performing. She'd savor the post gig cigarette in a couple of hours. She picked up her purse to lock it away for the night and heard the phone ringing. She dug into the bottom and retrieved it by the fourth ring. It was an unknown number.

Sliding the bar to answer, she said, "Hello?"

"Nique? It's me."

"Didi, I thought you were supposed to be off-line for at least a week." She knew this call wasn't approved. And there was no way this was going to be good.

"Yeah, well, I left the rehab place. Don't get mad, Nique. I have a better idea."

She pressed her lips together to keep from speaking. Wes was right. It was up to Didi to deal with this. If he wasn't ready, nothing she could say would make it work. She swallowed the tightness in her throat before it undid all her warming up.

"I saw some of the other people when I checked in, Nique. It was like a loony bin. I couldn't sleep. Someone is always screaming or moaning."

"What's the plan, Didi? You wanted to kick this, so what's the new plan?" She glanced at the clock. Tess would be calling them in a couple of minutes. "I've got to start the set soon." Why was he still able to talk so clearly? If he'd just left rehab, he should still be feeling the pain. As she thought the question through, Monique knew the answer – he was high.

"Okay, I heard about this rapid detox thing, like they can do it in a few hours, or maybe a day." He started coughing, and it turned into a fit. Finally getting control of it, he continued, "I called in a favor and I can go in tomorrow. It's a good plan, right?"

If he could get off the drugs fast, would it be better? "Who is doing you this favor? Are you sure it's legit?"

"Yeah it's Andy. You remember him? You'll never believe it. He was working in the clinic. He's a doctor. Who would have thought?"

Andy was Didi's best friend from elementary school. Monique had thought they were out of touch. "Yeah, I remember. Okay, where are you spending the night? Do you need my couch?" She would hope for the best with this and prepare for the worst.

"No, I don't want you to see me this way, Nique. Andy said I could crash at his place, and he'd take me in. Can you keep my stuff?"

"Of course. How do I get hold of you, Didi? Do you want your phone?" She assumed he had a phone in the bags he'd brought.

"No, Nique. I'll call you and leave Andy's number. If you need me, call him. I gotta go."

"Didi, before you go." Monique waited until Didi responded. "Tell me the truth. Did you know the guy across the hall from me?"

There was a pause before Didi said, "No. I swear."

He'd said those words too many times in the past for Monique to trust him, but it wasn't the time to argue. She'd wait until he was clean before she asked again. "Okay. Be careful, Didi. Remember what you told me. You don't want to go back to turning tricks right?"

"Yeah, Nique. I'll call you when I'm clean. Have a good show." His words were broken up as though he was shivering. Before she could ask, he ended the call.

Monique slid her phone back into her purse and locked it in the drawer. She pressed her hands into the desktop and blew out all the frustration she felt. Knowing she couldn't stop Didi from ruining his life didn't help her accept it. Drawing on the memory of the feeling she got when she sang, a feeling of power and purity, Monique put everything away that didn't help her sing. When she sang nothing could touch her.

"Ready?" Wes's voice settled over her with the first traces of calm.

"Right behind you. Let's go break some hearts."

5

Monique put the microphone on the stand as she let the last note fade. The warmth of the applause flowed over her. "That's it for tonight, friends. Order a new round and get ready for Dr. Jay and the Sliders. They'll be out in a few minutes. Good night and sweet dreams."

The set had done its magic. She was loose and ready for a late night. If she wasn't mad at Rafe, this was when she'd join him at his table, but he wasn't in the club. As it was, she wanted to stay here, have a drink, and enjoy the next set. If the guys wanted to leave, she'd sit at the bar by herself. She walked off stage as Ray played a few riffs on the piano.

Dr. Jay and his musicians were warming up in the back room, but they shifted into the hall to let Monique and the others collect their stuff.

"Anyone up for Dr. Jay's first set?" she asked, as she grabbed her cigarettes from her purse.

Wes pulled on his jacket. "Sorry, we have to go, early appointment." He packed his sax and followed Ray out.

"Ali?"

"I got a late gig at the Regent, sorry."

"No sweat. Have a great gig." She locked the drawer again, looking down so they couldn't see her disappointment. "See you next time."

The back door of the club was left unlocked so staff and entertainers could grab a smoke without mixing with the customers who indulged in front of the club. There was no handle on the outside of the door, so everyone propped it open with a rubber stop. The rain had stopped, leaving the alley filled with puddles, and the trash flattened into sodden mush. Monique lit up and stood under the overhang.

Now that it was time to leave, she realized why she wanted to stay. She didn't much want to go home to an empty apartment. It no longer felt like her haven. The murder wasn't the only thing that spoiled it. Anxiety about that creepy guy coming back was plucking at her nerves. And she was pissed off at Didi, but she would still worry about him. Unwinding with a couple of drinks was the best idea she had to smooth her nerves. When she was unwound, she'd go home and sleep.

She took the last drag and flicked the butt into a puddle. A glass of wine, maybe three, she was walking so it didn't matter how much she drank. Well, legally it didn't matter, but she wasn't stupid enough to get drunk and walk home.

The club was full, so Monique slid onto a stool at the end of the bar. A glass of red wine appeared in front of her before she had to ask. She nodded to Barry who was on shift tonight.

Letting the first sip linger on her tongue, Monique listened to the murmur of the crowd and waited for the sound to relax her. It was like meditation, something that let her release what was disturbing her soul. She was not going to think of Didi, or anything else.

Dr. Jay came on stage and started his patter. He liked to bring the audience into the act and they loved him for it. She ran her gaze around the room, now that she was off the stage, she could see everyone. One or two people met her eyes and raised a glass; they were her fans. She smiled back. It felt good to be appreciated with no strings attached.

One familiar face wasn't exactly a fan, and he was looking away from her, but Monique remembered him; Snake. One of Didi's buddies, a petty thief who kept trying to get Didi to join him on a job. As far as Monique knew, Didi had never said yes, but she couldn't be sure. She was turning away as someone joined Snake. Someone she knew, at least to recognize. Those black eyes had stared through the door at her yesterday.

Monique looked away, not wanting to be noticed. What was Snake into now? His thing was breaking into cars, shoplifting, and if he was telling the truth, committing a few break-and-enters.

Whatever Black Eyes was up to, it was far more serious than petty crime.

She wished she'd brought her purse with her, but it was still locked in the drawer. Without Watson's business card, even if she could borrow a phone, there was no way to call the cops without dialing 911 and causing a scene, and bringing his attention to her. No matter what her brain said about him not seeing her through the peephole, Monique couldn't quite get past the feeling he knew who she was.

The best she could do was watch. Maybe after Black Eyes left, she could talk to Snake, get some information for the cops.

Dr. Jay started to sing *Someone to Watch Over Me*; apparently it was creepy song night. Monique turned to look at the stage, keeping Snake's table in the corner of her sight. She gripped the edge of the bar to steady herself. The room suddenly chilly, her hand trembled, the wine rippling in response.

The two men huddled together and talked, paying no attention to the song, or anything else. She hazarded a peek at them over her wine glass. Both were dressed in black. Snake in jeans, tee shirt, and hoodie; Black Eyes in a leather jacket, dress pants, and shirt made out of some kind of shiny material. At their feet was a black gym bag. Monique was willing to bet it was the one from Alexi's apartment.

As she watched, Snake fumbled with something in his pocket, but at a word from his companion, he put his hands on the tabletop. Monique noticed a dirty bandage wrapped around Snake's left hand.

The conversation started again. Black Eyes was responding to Snake with a few clipped words. Snake looked like he was trying to wiggle out of something. He twitched every time the other man spoke, the signs of fear – or withdrawal symptoms. Was Snake tweaking?

Inside Monique felt the war between her real fear of what might be happening and a growing impulse to find out what had happened. There was more to what had happened than a simple murder. The violence she'd seen was extreme.

It was unfamiliar this feeling of curiosity. She'd never been the one to go seek justice. She always retreated from violence, even before her father... She pushed the memory back into the depths of her mind. Her head wanted to let it alone, to concentrate only on her current problems. She had enough of them to fill her mind. But whatever was going on seemed to be forcing itself into her life. She would pass this onto Watson as soon as she could get to the phone. All she was going to do was watch – gather intelligence. Snake could deal with his own problems.

As she tried to settle her internal argument, Megan, one of the waitresses, approached the table where Snake was starting to gesture at Black Eyes. The girl reached for an empty glass and Black Eyes grabbed her wrist, pushing her hand away from his drink.

Monique felt a shift, and the bar noise seemed to become muted. Barry started to move to the open end of the bar. One of the waiters, she thought his name was Ranjit, put his tray down on an empty table and stepped toward Megan. No one got rough with Tess's staff.

Megan looked over at the bar and shook her head, everyone relaxed.

Black Eyes must have felt the scrutiny – he snapped something at Snake and then released Megan's wrist. Snake pulled out his wallet and dropped a couple of bills on the table. They were sliding their chairs out, getting ready to take their conversation outside.

Monique beckoned to Barry as he finished pouring a martini for a customer. "Hey, keep my glass while I go for a smoke?"

Barry slid the half-empty glass of wine under the counter and moved on to the next order. Monique slipped out the front door just on the heels of Snake. He didn't notice her; his attention was on Black Eye's shoulders.

Outside there was a lineup of people waiting to get into the club, most of them chatting quietly. Another crowd of people were hanging around the streetlight, cigarettes in hand. Her quarry turned left onto a side street. Monique knew they might be heading for the free street parking and she would be seen if she followed, because there would be no one on the side streets at this time of night.

She hesitated. There was no doubt that being caught by Black Eyes would be bad, probably fatal. She told herself it would be just a peek around the corner. She wouldn't turn and go down the street, no matter what she saw. A peek as she passed, then she'd go back to the club, get her stuff from the lounge, call the police, and then finish her wine.

Behind her, she heard a few shouts of good night. Monique turned to see two couples head toward her. She stepped aside and let them pass. As soon as they were in front of her, Monique moved in behind and followed them, close enough to seem like she was part of the group to anyone watching, far enough that they didn't notice her.

The night was clear as only the end of a rainstorm could make it, the scent of moist earth drowning out the usual aroma of exhaust fumes and fast food. The chatter of the four people in front of her was familiar and made her feel safe. Monique had walked home in company of people just like this as often as she'd walked home alone.

Sometimes Tess softened up after a good night and would treat the staff to dinner and drinks. Even though dinner was pizza and drinks were the cheap stock brands, it was like family. The guys would insist on walking her home those nights. Other nights, Rafe would meet her and walk her home. If he'd been here, she wouldn't be chasing criminals. She might be arguing with him about it, but she'd be doing that in the safety of the club.

She pulled her jacket around her at the memory. She told herself that she didn't miss the feeling of being in a family. It had been a long time since she'd missed that. Family meant something different to her now.

Her cover group turned down the same street as Snake and Black Eyes. Monique realized the problem in her plan as she followed them. She couldn't see around the group. Moving onto the road, Monique used an SUV as cover to look down the street.

It had only been a minute, but there was no evidence of either man ahead of her. Monique wrapped her arms around her body, the cold suddenly sapping her strength and desire for the chase. One last look confirmed they were gone and it was time to go back to the club.

.　.　.

A FEW MINUTES LATER, Monique slid back onto her stool at the bar, reaching over she pulled her glass from under the counter. She soaked in the warmth of the club and told herself to stop getting involved in stuff that wasn't her business. She wouldn't call the cops. She had nothing to give them. Sure, Black Eyes had been here, but he was gone. The cops were on the case and they didn't need her help.

The wine did its job of relaxing her, and as Dr. Jay ended his set, she swallowed the last drop. The band was packing up and Tess had turned on the canned music. A few of the patrons called for their bills. The club would be empty in a half hour or so. Monique still wasn't ready to head home to her empty apartment, so she returned to the back room. A chat with Dr. Jay and a smoke would help her be ready.

"Hey, Monique," Dr. Jay said, his warm chocolate voice making her feel welcome. He was packing his trumpet into the case; usually he unpacked a couple of beers before leaving. "I hear you had a good set tonight."

"I heard your set and you make me sound like an amateur. You staying for a drink?" She unlocked the drawer and removed her purse. Flicking open her phone, Monique saw the new voicemail notification, Didi must have remembered to leave her the message with Andy's number.

"I gotta head to the airport. Joseph is coming in on the red eye. I said I'd pick him up." Joseph was Dr. Jay's son. He was going to school in Nova Scotia.

"Tell him I said hi." Monique pulled her cigarettes out of the bag. "Are the guys out back?"

Dr. Jay straightened, his trumpet case in hand. "No, they had a late gig to get to. You be careful now, Monique. See you on the B side." He headed out, leaving Monique alone in the room. She threw her bag over her shoulder and headed to the alley to have a cigarette before she asked if there was an after party in the club.

It was cool in the alley, but not as chill as it had been on the street. There was no wind in there. On hot days that meant a stink that turned her stomach. But tonight that meant a respite from the worst of the weather. As she took in the first lungful of smoke, Monique looked up at the sky. The moon was out of sight, but the night was so clear, she could still see a glow in the direction of downtown. Maybe things were going to get better. Maybe Didi would get clean. Maybe Rafe would stop pushing her to care more, maybe... screw it; maybe she should just enjoy the night.

The sound of footsteps made her draw back into the shadow of the door. Two people were entering the alley. She didn't often see anything here that wasn't a rat, or another smoker. Curiosity held her in the alley. A tingle of fear held her still when they started talking.

"But I can't just drop it off." Snake, whining as usual, stayed just out of view. "He'll want to know where I got it. I don't want to get him pissed at me."

Why had they come to the alley?

"I brought it because you said you would. Do as you said you would. Maybe we should have trusted your junkie friend? Maybe he would not be so afraid."

Snake had a lot of junkie friends. Monique told herself it didn't have to be Didi. She didn't recognize the voice but she guessed who it was. If he had been speaking to her, she wouldn't have argued, but it seemed Snake wasn't big on self-preservation.

"If you want me to take that chance, maybe I should get more money." His voice didn't carry any of the bravado of the words.

"No more money. We agreed on payment."

Monique licked her fingers and pinched the end of the cigarette to extinguish it and the telltale glow. Then she leaned fractionally out from the safety of the shadow. Snake was standing in a pool of light looking up at the other man.

The other man was Black Eyes. He was looking in the opposite direction from her so Monique felt safe. Monique slowly withdrew back into the shadow before either noticed her.

She still didn't have her phone. Not that she would have called from the alley, but she could have slipped inside the door and made the call, then back out to hear the rest.

There was no way she was going to miss whatever Black Eyes was going to say to Snake. She'd call Detective Watson later.

"But you didn't tell me what I had to do. Man, this is way outside my normal pay grade, you know what I mean?"

"No, I don't know what you mean. This is just for you to deliver the package to the location we agreed. This is no pay grade."

"But, he's already pissed off that Alexi took the bag. I tried to talk Alexi into giving it back, but he's not answering the phone."

Black Eyes snorted. "No, he won't be answering his phone again."

"Shit, he's dead? See, it's dangerous to have this thing."

"Only dangerous if you steal it."

Monique heard Snake mumble something but couldn't make out the words. There was definitely something more to this. There was no way that being paid to deliver a package, no matter who it was going to, would be that dangerous.

"What if he thinks I stole it? Does he know that Alexi was working alone?"

Stupid Snake, he might as well have said he was working with Alexi to start with.

"Is there reason for him to think you were involved?" Back Eye's voice was dangerously quiet.

"No, no reason at all." Monique heard real fear in Snake's voice this time. "How come you can't take it to him?"

Good question, Snake, perhaps there are a few brain cells left in your head.

"Don't ask questions. You do as you agreed."

"Uh, sure, sorry. I hope the cops don't follow me again."

Monique wondered what the hell was in the bag. Black Eyes didn't know he'd been seen picking it up, but he'd asked Snake to deliver it. None of this made sense. This mystery guy they were talking about was dangerous but the cops didn't know him? What the hell was this about?

"That would not be good." The words were flat, and Monique could hear the menace. "Why would police follow you?"

"I'm kind of a bad ass," Snake bragged. "I'm on their radar."

Monique heard a click in the silence that followed Snake's words.

"What the fuck, Vincent?" Snake's voice was high with fear. "I was just kidding around. I'll do it. I'll head over there now. No—"

His words were cut off with a gurgle.

"He knew you helped Alexi, stupid," Vincent hissed. "Now I have to tell him he won't get to kill you." Then she heard calm footsteps retreat to the street.

When she was sure that Vincent was gone, Monique hurried to where Snake was collapsed face down on the ground. She flipped him onto his back and then rocked away, clutching her stomach to stop herself retching.

Snake's throat was slit from one side to the other. She could see flesh and cartilage torn raggedly apart. As she watched, a mist of red floated from the gash. Then Snake gurgled one last time.

6

Scrambling to her feet, trying to avoid the blood she now saw mixing with the puddles, Monique ran for the door to the club. Snake was beyond help, but now she had information that she could give the police. And she had to do it fast. The blackness was crawling in from the edge of her sight.

The sound of people laughing in the club as she ran down the hall to the lounge seemed out of place. She thought about going in and telling everyone but tossed the idea aside. The police first, then whoever was still around.

She fumbled with the lock on the drawer and dropped the key when she saw the red stain smeared on it. Her hands were sticky with Snake's blood. Looking down she saw, then felt, the dampness of her clothes. It didn't matter. She'd clean up later. If she stopped now, she would curl up into a ball. She had to think of the blood as evidence, or something else. If she thought of it as blood, she'd be useless. The blackness would take over and she would be too far gone to help.

Monique knew she wasn't responsible for Snake's death, but if she'd just thought to call the cops earlier, he might be alive. He was a whiny petty thief, but he didn't deserve to die like that.

Finally getting the drawer open, Monique dug out her phone and Detective Watson's business card. Everything stuck to her hands. She would have to get a new phone. Even if she cleaned it, she'd remember that feeling, the stickiness, and the smell.

She closed her eyes. It was no point letting her thoughts get in the way. She knew this feeling, knew that she'd be incoherent soon. Knew that she had a short time to tell them what happened before it all came crashing down. Her hands trembled, but she managed to press the numbers.

"Watson."

She blurted out the words before she could think about it. "Detective Watson, it's Monique Duchesne. I'm at Blue Scene. There's been a murder in the back alley. You need to get here."

"Slow down, Monique. What happened?"

"Just come. The alley opens onto Main. You'll see what happened. There is a lot of blood."

He spoke to someone on the other end. Then, to her, "We're on the way. Are you sure the person is dead?"

"Snake, it's Snake. I think his real name is Paul Reed, or something." She could feel the darkness pushing harder at her senses. "Yes, he's dead."

"Did you see what happened?"

"Yes. How long before you get here?"

"Do you know who did it?"

"How long?"

"Where are you? Exactly?"

"In the lounge. In the musician's lounge."

"Stay there. We'll be five minutes."

Monique ended the call. She needed to lie down, to get blood back to her head because the darkness was pressing harder. She couldn't let it win this time. She wouldn't pass out. What if she never woke up?

"Monique! My god what happened?" Tess's voice broke through the cycle of panic. "Are you hurt?"

Tess took Monique's arms in a tight grip, as though she could stop her from slipping into unconsciousness just by holding her. It worked. The blackness receded a fraction and Monique felt something more than panic and cold.

Monique blinked. Why was Tess angry? Oh, yeah. "I'm sorry. I tried not to get the blood everywhere. I'll clean it."

"We'll worry about that later. Is this your blood?" Tess's hands started to feel at Monique for evidence of wounds. "If someone hurt you, they'll answer to me."

Monique pushed herself into a sitting position. "No, it's not me. It's Snake. He's in the alley."

"Okay. I guess something caught up with him finally. I'll call an ambulance and get him taken care of." Tess made to stand.

"No. He doesn't need an ambulance," Monique said as she tried to wipe the blood off her arms. "The cops are on their way. I called them."

A flash of irritation crossed Tess's face, and then her expression returned to concern. "Okay, we'll deal with it. Maybe it'll bring the club some business – people will do the weirdest things for the most morbid reasons."

It made Monique feel more comfortable when Tess was all business. There was something wrong about a Tess who cared.

She took Monique's wrist and tugged. "Stop rubbing your arms. You're just spreading the blood. I'll send Barry to the back door so he can let the cops in. I'll be back."

Monique touched her face. She could feel dried blood like a second skin. She was going to need a shower and clean clothes – and soon. The smell was starting to turn her stomach. The blackness still lurked at the edge of her senses.

Tess marched into the room, placing a pile of clean bar towels on the chair and a bucket of hot soapy water on the floor.

"I've told everyone to stay out. You can wash in this, and I'll find you something to wear from the lost and found. It won't be great, but it will be better than what you are wearing. Stay like that and it won't be long before you start attracting flies."

"Thanks," Monique said as she started to remove her clothes.

"No problem." Tess put a spray bottle of disinfectant on the chair beside the towels. "Use some of the cloths to clean the desk and the floor before it stains too badly. Chuck the dirty towels in the trash. I'll take the cost out of your pay."

Monique waited until she was alone and then stripped off her bloody clothes. She was grateful for the warm water. Shivering in her bra and panties, she dunked her hands into the water feeling the crusty blood breaking as it got wet.

She made quick work of cleaning herself and was getting ready to spray the desk when Tess opened the door. "Put this on." She threw a tee shirt at Monique. "The cops are here. I told them to wait until you were ready."

Alone again, Monique pulled the tee shirt over her head. It was long enough to cover her to mid-thigh. By the time she was able to go home, it would be freezing outside. It wouldn't be enough, but maybe she wouldn't have to walk home. She'd swallow her objections and take a ride from the cops. Monique pushed her clothes into the trashcan, knowing she would never want to wear them again.

She suddenly started to tremble. Telling herself it was adrenaline, she tried to spray the desk with disinfectant. It wasn't accurate, but it would do. The trembling eased as she cleaned the blood out of the room and the smell went from coppery blood to clean pine.

Two minutes later, Detective Watson walked into the musician's lounge and seemed to fill the room with his authority. Monique was curled up in the biggest chair waiting for him.

Arms wrapped around herself to stop the shivering – or trembling, she wasn't sure which.

"You look like you could use a drink," he said.

"I just want to get this over with." Monique wanted her bed, and her own wine, and her own clothes, and a hot shower. She didn't care what order they came in.

"The team is dealing with the crime scene. I need to talk to you about what happened."

He barely looked at her while he spoke. He inspected the lounge like it was a crime scene. Monique uncurled. "Do you want to take my statement here?"

He turned his gaze back to her. "No, at the station. I'll take you home to change first. It wouldn't be good for you to freeze to death in custody."

Monique almost refused the offer, a knee jerk reaction. She remembered her thoughts a few minutes ago, and decided she needed clothes more than she wanted to be done with the cops. Maybe she could get a shower too if he wasn't in a hurry. "Okay." She pulled herself up and looked at her shoes. They were soaked. "How far is your car?"

He saw where she was looking. "It's out front. You can leave the shoes here. Did you throw your clothes into the trash? We need them for evidence."

Monique nodded then shoved her shoes into the garbage bag before following him through the club. It looked like Tess had sent everyone home. She was waiting at the bar. A shot of whiskey in front of her. "You need a lawyer, Monique?"

Monique looked at Watson. He'd mentioned her being in custody, but there was no way he could think she killed Snake. "I don't think so, Tess. Thanks anyway. If anything changes, I have someone I can call."

The drive to her apartment was only a few minutes, but it went by in silence, and felt like an age. Monique kept her eyes on the passing scenery, stopping her mind from squirreling into the details of Snake's death.

When they arrived at her apartment, Monique told Detective Watson she'd be taking a shower and didn't wait for the answer. She stood under the stream until the water scalded her skin bright pink. Then she scrubbed the last traces of blood from her skin, traces real and imagined. The steam followed her into her bedroom where she dug out an old pair of jeans and a pale blue tee shirt. The soft cotton touching her skin felt like a caress of comfort.

When she came back to the living room, Detective Watson handed her a bowl of cereal. "You need to eat, and we don't have anything healthy at the station. You don't have much either, but this is better than nothing."

She didn't feel like eating, but he was right. She couldn't remember her last meal and she didn't need to pass out when she gave her statement.

Show no sign of weakness. She'd learned that lesson years ago.

She finished the cereal, tipped the bowl to drink the sweet-ened milk, and then, with a nod at Watson, she picked up her purse. "Let's get this over with."

DETECTIVE WATSON SHOWED Monique into a small windowless room. There was a smell that she couldn't quite identify, stale, sour, and unpleasant. It brought unwanted memories to her mind. She sat on a metal chair opposite Watson facing a large mirror that she knew was a one-way window. "Should I have taken Tess up on her offer of a lawyer?"

He shook his head. "This is all we have for privacy. Sorry it's not that comfortable."

"Why couldn't we do this at my place?" The food and shower

had helped drive away the shock of hearing Snake's murder, and seeing his life drain out with the flow of blood. Monique was realizing that perhaps Watson had been playing good cop up to now, but this time she'd fallen for it. Letting her get clean and feeding her could just have been a technique to disarm her. She tried to ignore the twinge of disappointment, because she'd fallen for it, and because it wasn't real.

Watson took out his notebook and placed it on the table next to him. "You've been at the scene of two brutal murders in two days. I think a bit of formality is called for."

Monique waited for him to continue, unwilling to share information without specific questions.

"Tell me what you saw tonight?" He flipped open the notebook and held his pen ready.

Monique rubbed her face to try to remove the pain from the memory. There had been so much blood. She took a breath and then laid out the facts of what happened. "Then I called you," she finished.

"How do you know this Snake?"

"A friend of my brother."

"Your brother's name?"

"Why?"

"We need to gather all the details."

Monique didn't think it would do any good to argue. She gave Didi's name.

"How did he become a friend of Snake?"

"I don't know."

"This isn't the first time you've been at the scene of a crime."

Her stomach tightened. This was what she'd been dreading. "No, but that doesn't have anything to do with this."

"It might. I did some digging after yesterday. You seem to have overcome your past, your brother not so much."

Monique clenched her hands. Why did he ask about Didi if

he already knew? He had no right to dig into her past. She was a witness not a suspect. Then there was that sympathetic look that everyone got. "Didi was young. I had to deal with it for his sake. We did okay."

"It couldn't have been easy. Getting through what you saw. Your mother stabbed. Your father shot through the head."

"Do you think I had a choice?"

Monique remembered that day as if it were happening in front of her. She'd come home three days after her eighteenth birthday. Her first paycheck in her hands. Proud to show her father she was self-sufficient. When she opened the door, Monique knew something was wrong from the sickly, bloody stench. Even before she saw the source, she felt the pain of loss.

She just hadn't anticipated the betrayal. She stopped at the kitchen door, seeing pools of blood, and pieces of what she learned later were brain and bone. Her mother was sprawled in front of the refrigerator a carving knife sticking out of her belly, moving up and down as she gasped her last breaths through a hole in her throat. Monique had run to her mother, praying that she could help. Her last breath had rasped out through bloody bubbles as Monique reached for her.

Her father was unrecognizable, half of his head blown away. She ran out of the house screaming. A neighbor called the police. Monique told them someone must have broken in. Some stranger must have killed her parents. The whole time she protested, the sight of the gun just outside her father's grasp told her what had really happened.

Her father had killed her mother and then himself.

There had been no warning, no apparent reason. Even after a deep investigation, no one understood what had turned her loving father into a killer.

Detective Watson's voice brought her back to the present. "No. I guess you didn't. You got help, right?"

Monique nodded. "Victim's services made sure I had counseling. I had to make sure Didi was taken care of. He was in care. I..." She realized he had gotten her talking when she meant to keep silent. "Do you need anything else from me?"

He looked like he wanted to say something more, but he just finished making notes on a pad of paper. "Let me confirm some of these details. You didn't know what was going to happen, but you listened to the threats being made?"

Monique nodded.

"You didn't think to call us based on what you heard?"

"I did, but I didn't think it would go that far. And I didn't have my phone with me. I thought I would hear something that would help you find that Alexi guy's killer."

"You heard this Snake call the killer Vincent. Did you hear a last name?"

Monique shook her head.

"You didn't hear what this mystery man's name was?"

"No. I told you what I heard. They were both afraid of him whoever he is."

"Do you know what was in the bag?"

"I would have told you if I did. It was something heavy, but it didn't make any noise, just like I told you when I called about the break-in."

Watson made more notes.

"Do you need anything else from me?" Monique was going to ask for a lawyer if they made her stay any longer. The questions didn't make any sense. She'd been clear with her answers, and Watson seemed to be making more out of it than a witness statement.

Watson looked up from his notebook and then tucked the pen inside. "No, we'll get you a ride home. If we need to talk to you again, we know how to find you. Unless you're planning to go on vacation?"

"You can find me at work or at home. You have my number." She gathered her things. She couldn't help feeling he suspected her. Like she was so damaged by what her father had done, she was suddenly murdering strangers. Or perhaps there was some genetic drive to murder that she'd inherited. Maybe something that got triggered at the age of thirty-six. "I can get a cab. You don't need to send me home in a cruiser."

Even at one in the morning, it would raise some eyebrows if she were dropped off at home by a police cruiser. She didn't want to have to deal with the suspicious looks. And the unasked questions of her neighbors would haunt her every time they passed in the lobby. They usually left her alone, and that's how she liked it.

7

Monique lay flat on her back diagonally across her bed. The room was dark. She had blackout blinds because it was usual for her to be sleeping during the day.

She should be asleep. She should be exhausted, but instead she was wide-awake. The events of the last two days had drained her of anything like normal feelings. She didn't know how to turn it off, the energy, or the adrenalin. The reminder of her father's crime wasn't new. It ran through her dreams at least three times a month. The rerun of that day keeping her stuck in this empty half-healed place. Part of her wanted to remember, and a bigger part wanted to forget completely.

The cops seemed more interested in her history than in the current crimes. She couldn't shake the feeling that Watson was going to try to prove she'd committed them. That she'd had a psychotic break because of her history. It didn't surprise her. After all, she worried that she'd do something like that. That she could have inherited whatever had caused her father to do what he'd done. And that got added to the guilty feeling that Didi might have turned out differently if he hadn't lost his parents.

That she might have turned out differently...That she could have done something...

If Didi was involved in this mess, she didn't know what she would do. He wouldn't have a chance in jail. He'd be back on drugs and turning tricks before the first week was out.

A car door slammed across the street. Monique jumped to peek through her blinds.

What if it was Black Eyes – Vincent? What if he was coming to finish the job, get rid of the witnesses. She slid the blinds back an inch and glanced at the road.

She focused on the man standing beside a black SUV, tall and thin, he could be Vincent. Then he stepped into the circle of light from the streetlamp. Black, he was black, and young – not a danger. Monique swallowed her fear and slid back onto the bed.

This was crazy.

This would make her crazy if she didn't do something. The most useful something would be sleep so she could get perspective. Monique lay on her back and closed her eyes, even though the room was dark, closing her eyes helped her focus. She tried to tell her body to relax, but as she started the normal exercise, she realized her muscles weren't tense. She was just awake, not keyed up. She switched to convincing herself that she was asleep. Breathing slowly, running a dream of walking in a forest through her mind.

She recognized the symptoms of sleep creeping in and tried not to acknowledge them. She slipped into a shallow doze, trying to ignore the knowledge that she was sleeping.

The stairwell door slammed. Her heart stopped beating. A woman's voice giggled drunkenly. Mac was home.

She blew out a breath to dispel the shock. Telling herself it wasn't a threat, or rather not a physical one. It meant she wasn't going to get any sleep by lying on the bed. Monique decided it was time to do the one thing that was not supposed to be good for her sleep problems, lying on the couch with a boring TV show.

TWENTY MINUTES LATER, Monique gave up. It was getting too close to morning to waste time trying to force her body to sleep when it didn't want to. She didn't have to sing tonight, so it wouldn't matter all that much if she didn't get a good night's sleep.

If she called Rafe, there would just be a new fight, one that might be enough to drive them apart permanently. And she wasn't ready for that. She was too raw from the police station to try to solve any other problems. And even thinking about it gave her the feeling that Rafe was right, she didn't let anyone in unless she needed something. No. She had to deal with this herself.

Monique paced, desperately wanting to find something to pass the lonely hours. At the door, she looked through the peephole, something that was getting to be a familiar action.

Alexi's apartment looked normal. Except for the police tape, there was no evidence of what had happened. No bloody hand marks, no broken locks. She wondered if the landlord had cleaned the mess. Was there going to be a new tenant?

She dragged herself away from the door and started to tidy the apartment. Returning the pillows to her bed, straightening the throw on the couch, and sorting the DVDs into alphabetical order took five minutes. Monique glanced at Didi's bags, fingers itching to sort the contents, conscience bothered at the thought she really just wanted to snoop.

Returning to the peephole, she studied the door. If the apartment was like hers, there was only a simple lock, no deadbolt. There was still no seal on the door other than the drape of police tape, and no extra lock from the police. Maybe she could get the door open somehow and look around. Maybe they forgot to set the lock when the cops finished. Maybe there was some clue to the identity of the guy Snake was talking about.

Maybe she could find something to get the police off her back and onto a real trail.

She turned the handle on her door and pulled it open a crack. No sound from Mac's place. At least tonight he was getting some sleep. Would it help if she was more like him? Loose and ready to take on any opportunity. The three apartments at the other end of the hall were occupied by people who went to work, watched TV, and went out on the weekend. In other words, normal people.

Slipping across the hall, she turned the doorknob. No luck. There was still no sound of activity in any of the apartments, so Monique took a chance, twisting the knob and then jiggling it. Still no luck. It gave her some sense of security that her apartment was harder to get into than she worried it was. It didn't make up for the frustration of not getting into Alexi's place.

Voices came from one of the apartments at the other end. They were getting ready to leave for work. She remembered the guy, Ethan, boring her with talk about arbitrage and world markets, blah blah blah. If they were leaving this early, there must be a stock exchange open somewhere in the world.

Monique ran for her apartment and shut the door, leaning her back against it while her heart slowed to a normal pace. She was not going to let a simple lock get between her and finding out some information on this murder. She knew that it made no sense that she would be able to find a clue. That she could do what the police – the professionals – couldn't, but this felt purposeful. It was something that she could do and not just worry about. She would just check it out. She only needed to get through the door.

If Didi were available, she would call him. He knew how

to break into places. He'd learned how so he could support his habit. She didn't know if he ever actually stole anything, and she didn't ask. But Didi wasn't available, and she was not going to ask him for help and give him an excuse to avoid detox. Her glance took in the bags again. If he really had packed all his belongings, there would be lock picks in there. She could figure out how to use them, all she needed was time.

Placing the bags on the table, she started removing the contents. There were clothes, all needing a good cleaning. She dragged her hamper out of the bedroom and started filling it with his clothes after carefully checking the pockets for anything that wouldn't survive a wash, or he wouldn't need after detox.

At the bottom of the first bag, she found a bundle of Mole-skine notebooks wrapped in a plain elastic band. She placed it to the side without snooping. A package of condoms, and the business card for an acupuncturist were the last things she took from there. The second bag contained more clothes. In the pocket of one pair of jeans, Monique found the leather wallet containing his picks.

The only thing she knew about using them was one went into the lock first and the other wiggled stuff around. She was going to need some time to practice.

The hall was clear again. Monique figured she had at least an hour until someone else got up or came home. She tried to remember when the other neighbors made noise in the morning. She flushed with embarrassment when she realized she didn't know. Was that normal? Maybe it was for someone who worked nights and slept days.

It didn't matter now. If she was going to start being normal, she'd do it as soon as she solved this.

It felt like it was much later, but it was only getting on for 3 am and the clubs closed at four. If anyone was out, they were out for a while.

She fingered the picks and tried to remember anything she knew about locks. They were made up of tumblers and disks... that sounded right. The idea was to align the pins, that's what a key did, moved the pins up in the right pattern.

Monique took the picks and her keys and stepped across the hall. Juggling the tools in her fingers, Monique eyed the lock. The one that looked like an Allen key probably was like a lever, she put the short end in the bottom of the keyhole and tried to turn. It moved a little. She took a thin rod that actually looked like a pick and slid it into the lock. It went all the way through. She tried to turn the lock, but it didn't move.

"Okay, I guess it shouldn't be that simple."

She cocked an ear to make sure she wasn't about to be interrupted, and then looked at the lock again. She used the thin pick to feel around inside. Things shifted upward as she did. Hope brought a smile to her lips. She slid the pick to the back of the lock and pushed upward on everything she felt until she pulled out the pick. The Allen key fell out of the lock.

"Fuck!" Monique slid the Allen key back into the lock and then turned. It didn't go anywhere.

She took in a deep breath and removed the two metal probes. Looking at her key, she realized that the problem was too much space between the piece she used to push the pins and the bottom of the channel.

She started again, this time inserting the long end of the Allen key piece and using it to hold the pick against the pins as she pushed them up. This time it felt different, pushing up on the pick she felt the pins lock. When she felt the last pin rise up, she kept the pressure on the pick as she turned it. The two metal probes moved together like a key. She kept twisting, suddenly the door unlocked and opened a few inches.

Monique slipped inside Alexi's apartment before anyone could notice.

The apartment was dark, but she knew there was a light switch near her hand. She hesitated. The smell was foul, and she knew that no one had cleaned up after the crime. Bob, her landlord, would have a fit. This place was not getting rented out for a long time. Steeling herself, Monique flicked on the lights, keeping her gaze on the floor.

She knew she had to look, there was no point in being there if she didn't. She just needed to take a second before going forward. Telling herself that she wasn't going to freak out, she raised her eyes. The living room carpet was stained brownish red. She could hear the buzz of flies, but tried not to see them, or the stain.

Vincent had come through this mess to find the bag. She could do it. She needed to do it. Monique took a path near the wall to avoid stepping in the sticky mess. Looking at the walls didn't help much because blood had splashed across the paint, but it was enough to help her stay on the sane side of crazy.

She stepped into the kitchen and opened cupboards and drawers finding nothing helpful, just a lot of grime. The bathroom was no better. In fact, it looked like Alexi had never cleaned. The medicine cabinet held prescription bottles made out to different patients. He was obviously well diversified in his crimes, stealing from other criminals, and selling prescription drugs.

The bedroom was across the apartment. Across the pool of blood. Monique, already breathing shallowly, put her hand over her mouth and held her breath as she scurried around the room to the half open door.

She turned on the light and closed the door behind her.

The room had been tossed. The mattress, thrown off the bed, was leaning against the bureau. A hole cut in the center of the box spring large enough to have held the bag. The drawers of the bureau were broken and scattered across the floor. If there was something here before Vincent got in, it was gone.

Monique started to shake. She breathed out and tried to stop the panic attack by clenching her fists. The tension transferred the tremors to her legs, and her strength left her. She collapsed into a crouch. She couldn't get enough air into her lungs, but with each shallow breath she tasted copper and rot.

She had to get out of the apartment. She couldn't pass out here.

Monique pushed herself up. Still shaking, she stumbled on the first step and leaned a hand against the wall to steady herself. Counting to five, she took another step and then another. She remembered to turn off the light as she left. She continued to shuffle around the mess until she reached the door to the apartment. Turning the final light off as she lurched through the door, Monique made it back to her apartment, locking the door behind her as she gasped in lungs full of clean air.

—————

8

Monique sank to the floor, her arms around her legs, face pressed into her knees. Her whole body wracked with the shakes. Eventually her gasps for clean air slowed, turning into deep sobs. She hadn't felt this broken for years.

It was like fate had held onto all of these experiences, deciding to serve them up one after the other in some kind of warped banquet, to see if she would break. Today she'd seen a violent murder, been reminded of her parent's death, and seen the remnants of another violent end. It was too much. If she could only sleep, maybe it would feel more distant, more like something she could handle.

She knew self-pity wasn't a good place to spend time. She'd learned that at eighteen. Tears hadn't changed anything then. It hadn't brought her mother back. The only way anyone could get through this kind of thing was to push away the emotions and get on with life.

Didi still needed her. She still had to make enough money to pay her bills. Keeping her expectations low meant she didn't face too many disappointments.

The sobs subsided, and the tremors that rocked her body faded into a strung out feeling that just left her cold and empty. Stiff from the panic attack and the cold floor, Monique forced her muscles into action. Wiping her eyes with her fingers, she shrugged off the last of the turmoil in her mind.

Tea would help. Well, tequila would help more right now, but hiding in a substance-induced peace was how Didi dealt with things. Monique knew that it didn't help in the long run. It just added another problem to the growing wall of obstacles to living a normal life. Monique never wanted to fall that far, she had sworn she'd survive her past, not be defined by it. She needed to be strong so Didi knew there was a place up from the bottom.

The simple task of filling the kettle and waiting for the water to boil helped her to move further away from the memory and shock. Despite the pain, Monique swore she was going back to that apartment. Less sure that there would be a clue, she needed to know she'd done all she could to solve this murder. Maybe doing that would help to heal the scar over her past.

Monique knew in her bones that figuring out Alexi's murder would solve Snake's, and that would get the cops off her back. She needed sleep. She needed to prepare herself. She needed rest, but not for long.

The reaction to the blood had drained the last dregs of energy from her. But the tea worked its magic releasing the tightness in her muscles. She poured more hot water over the teabag and took it to the living room. Placing the mug on her coffee table, she reflected on the difference between her home and Alexi's. Not all the mess had been from his death. The man had lived like a pig, wallowing in garbage and disarray. The blood had added a layer of evil to an already squalid life.

Monique rolled herself in the throw and closed her eyes. A half hour of sleep would still give her time before everyone else started their day. There would be plenty of time to search the apartment and recover from the inevitable reaction. She felt sleep drape across her consciousness.

THE PHONE RANG, ripping Monique from her dreams. Part of her was relieved, the dreams were not happy ones, and part was furious, she needed the sleep. More than that, she realized, she needed sleep that wasn't tortured with dreams of death, and pain, and betrayal.

Monique checked the time as she answered her phone, 3:30 am. She'd had twenty minutes rest.

She didn't check the caller ID. "Yes?"

"Nique, did I wake you? I'm sorry."

"It's okay, Didi. What do you need?" She crossed her fingers that he was still at Andy's and he wasn't calling for money. She couldn't ask the one question that screamed from her mind. If Didi said he was involved with the people who killed Alexi, she wouldn't know what to do, how to help him.

"Just to talk. I'm kind of scared, Nique."

She sat up ready for the worst. "Have you been using?"

"I had to, Nique. I can't be in withdrawal when I go in. Don't freak, I got it legit. And it was my last time, by tonight I'll be clean."

It couldn't be that easy. If it were, there wouldn't be any addicts left. "It will be out of your system, Didi, that's only part of it."

"Yeah I know. I gotta deal with the head stuff. But, at least, I won't be puking and sweating for days. That's the hard part."

She wished she could let him think that. "Didi, you've tried kicking it before. This isn't the hard part. It's just the physical part." No matter what happened in the detox, Didi would have to deal with why he was addicted. She knew why he needed to get away from reality, it was the same reason she panicked at the sight of blood. He just needed to figure out why he turned to drugs instead of something else. The memory of the withdrawals hadn't kept him clean, but maybe this detox would give him a chance.

"Yeah, I know. Nique, I don't want to talk about it. I just need to talk about anything else. What were you doing? I called a while ago and you didn't answer."

Fuck! Monique hadn't noticed the missed call. "I was out." She didn't want to tell him that Snake was dead, or that she'd been questioned.

"You sound weird."

Why did he suddenly have to get perceptive? "I had a problem with the apartment across the hall."

"The murdered guy's place? What kind of problem?"

What could she say? He wasn't going to give up, so she had to say something. "I thought I could find a clue. The cops don't seem to be doing anything about it."

"It's not your problem, Nique." His annoyance at her was plain. "You could get hurt." No longer worried about the detox, he was in brother mode. He didn't get much chance to act it, but when he did, Didi tried on the big brother role not his real one. It didn't work, but Monique was warmed by the fact he could let go of his own problems for a while.

"I got in, Didi. I figured out your lock picks." Would he be deflected from concern? Could she get him interested in the problem?

He grunted – maybe a laugh. "Good for you. Are you planning on using that skill in your spare time?"

Monique smiled. "No."

"So did you find a clue?"

"No. It was a mess. I didn't stay long."

Didi sighed. "You should have called me. I would have helped you. I could have picked the lock. I could have—"

"Didi, you need to get yourself ready for detox. I didn't want to bring you into it. I was fine." She bit her lip to stop speaking. Too many assurances would make him more suspicious. "It's fine."

"I don't believe you." There was a pause long enough that Monique wondered if Didi was going to speak again. He finally broke the silence to say, "Okay, so you are fine. Why do you think you need to find a clue?"

"You are acting very reasonable, Didi. Should I worry about that?"

He snorted. "Give me a break. You keep telling me I should grow up and now that I am acting like an adult you get suspicious."

Monique felt the rush of anger. "Why is it always about you, Didi? Are you going to tell me I have no reason to be suspicious? How many times have you lied to me?"

"About as many times as you lied to me." Didi ground out the words. Monique imagined him clenching his teeth in anger like he'd done since he was old enough to do more than just scream out his fury.

She wasn't letting him off the hook, though. "I only ever lied to you to protect you. You lied to me about using, about stealing. You lied to me to protect your addiction."

"The difference is I believed your lies. You never trusted me enough to believe." The familiar whine soured his voice.

Monique heard all the years of the drugs talking through Didi's voice. It burned her like a hot poker shoved into her guts. Heroin ruined her life because it stole Didi's. Addiction soiled everything around the addict. Her brother had been a happy kid. That ended in one vicious unexplained act eighteen years ago. "I used to trust you. It wasn't me who broke the trust, Didi."

"Fuck you, Nique. I called because I wanted to talk to you before I went in for this thing. I thought you would care that I was trying. I'm scared because maybe I could die. But don't worry. I won't bother you. Maybe I'll let you know how it goes."

Hearing the words doused her anger. If something happened to Didi – she didn't want to think about it. For all his faults, he was her only family. "Didi, I'm sorry. I'm tired I shouldn't have said that... Didi?"

"Yeah, sure. Take care, Nique." Didi ended the call.

Monique threw her phone onto the table. The tiny amount of rest she'd gotten from the nap was gone. She knew he wouldn't take her call if she phoned back, and she had no idea where Andy lived, so she could only hope Didi would call as soon as he was done with the detox. He never held a grudge. That was her personality fault. In fact, she remembered that until he was hooked, he rarely fought with her. He had been quiet and calm. She hadn't known that he was hiding as much hurt inside as she was. Monique thought that keeping him from seeing the scene would somehow stop him from being damaged by it.

She tossed the throw onto the end of the couch and paced between the kitchen and living room. There was no way she could ease herself into another nap. It wouldn't do any good returning to the other apartment until she dealt with the residual anger from the argument. Even the thought of facing the blood made her lightheaded. That shot of tequila was looking more tempting. Thank god she was too smart to keep hard liquor at home. Working in a bar gave her the opportunity for an occasional indulgence, and that was enough.

She knew what she needed to do. Reluctant as she was, talking to Rafe was the right thing. If she called him, that would be one less argument hanging out there. Making peace with Rafe would give her the strength to go back in that apartment.

She couldn't let that go either. There were too many threads hanging loose in her life. It was time to start tucking some of them into the fabric again.

Rafe would probably be awake and working. There was no point in delaying her apology any longer. With everything else that was going on, their argument seemed childish, and the easiest of all the problems to fix. She curled up on the couch and called him.

"Hi, Monique, what's up?"

That wasn't very encouraging. She'd been hoping for something more like, *I've missed you.* "Didi is going into rapid detox today." There was a pause after her abrupt speech. Monique wondered if Rafe could sense there was so much more to tell. She didn't want to dump all her problems on his lap. He already thought she was using him, no need to reinforce that idea.

Rafe finally spoke, "It's a better way to get the poison out of him. I wrote an article about it last month. Some addicts don't make it through the other way. Are you going with him?"

"He doesn't want me to. He's kind of mad at me right now."

Rafe grunted in understanding, whether that was of her or Didi, Monique couldn't tell. She waited again for his response, feeling as though she was passing through a series of tests. If she said the right thing, Rafe would listen to her again. If she said the wrong thing, then she wasn't sure what they would do next.

"What happened?"

Monique told him, "I should have kept my mouth shut."

"Was it the truth?"

Monique wondered the same thing. She'd trusted Didi all the way up to the time she found out that he'd lied about drugs. Since then she was always waiting for the lies to show their ugly heads. No matter what Didi said, she thought he was hiding something. She never knew if it was the addiction or her brother talking. "Yes, but I didn't need to say it."

"The truth is better for him than another lie. Monique, this isn't your fault. He's scared and being mad at you is better than worrying about his immediate future. You know that addicts don't always react like people. Sometimes it's the addiction. Do you want me to come over?"

It was tempting to say yes, but then she wouldn't be able to go into Alexi's apartment again. If she didn't go back tonight, Monique wasn't sure she'd have the courage to do it another time. "No, I'm fine." It was true. Hearing his voice had settled something inside her.

"I can tell you aren't. What else happened?"

Monique found herself reluctant to talk about Snake, or the police, or breaking into the apartment. "Nothing."

"Fine, you want Didi to be honest with you. Maybe you should try the same approach." His words didn't contain any annoyance. It was like a teacher pointing out a lesson. That almost made it worse. If he didn't care enough to argue with her, maybe it was too late for them to have a future.

Monique blew out her breath and decided that telling him wouldn't be any worse than keeping it in. "I saw someone get murdered."

"Christ, Monique. How can you say nothing else happened?"

She could feel tears burn her eyes and tighten her throat. Monique swallowed and answered in a small voice, "I think the cop suspected me. He knew about my dad."

"That's shitty, babe. I'm coming over. You don't have to deal with this alone."

"No!" Monique knew Rafe would stop her from going next door, and she had to do it. She had to do it alone because she couldn't go through life afraid of violence, and she couldn't live with the threat of being accused of murder. If the press got interested in this story, her history would be all over the papers, and news, and probably the Internet. How would Didi survive that?

How would she? "I'm going to sleep. I just didn't want to miss you anymore."

"Monique, stop doing that." His words were barked out like an order. Not like him at all.

Monique wondered if she would ever be able to have a conversation with someone she loved that didn't turn into a fight. At any hint there was going to be a disagreement, and she felt herself push back. "Doing what?" she asked fully aware of what he meant.

"You know damn well. Anytime we get into it you shut me down."

There was no way she would be able to talk about this now. She knew that it was a familiar feeling, and there never seemed to be a time when she could talk about it. "I'm just tired. It's been a long day. Let it be, Rafe, please." She knew it was a futile request.

"You can't draw a line around your world, Monique. If you want me to be part of your life, you need to let me in."

Stomach clenching in fear of his next words, Monique couldn't stop herself from saying, "If you didn't want to be in every aspect of my life, it would be easier to let you into part of it."

"Are you sure you want me in your life at all?" His voice was dangerously low. "It's like you've created a map of your world. You are inside the borders of Monique Country and everything else is outside, standing with the dragons, in *Terra Incognito*."

"That's not true. I have plenty of people in my life." She wished that didn't sound so plaintive.

"No. You have plenty of people standing on the border, willing to be in your life. But you don't let anyone in. People who love you don't want to be in part of your life. They want to be in all of it."

Tears flowed, and Monique told herself they were from frustration, not from hearing the truth. "Didi is in my life, and you are."

"You don't even realize it, do you? Didi is only in your life as long as he needs you to rescue him. If he does manage to overcome his demons, you'll push him away."

"Are you saying I don't want Didi to get clean? Of course I do."

"You are so missing the point, Monique. Yes, of course you want him to get clean. You need to ask yourself if that's because you love him, or because then he won't be a burden. If he can take care of himself, you can push him to the edge of Monique Country with the rest of us."

Wiping her face on her sleeve, Monique tried to calm down. Rafe knew why she was like this. He knew her history. It had taken a lot of guts for her to tell him when she realized their relationship was going to linger – courage and a fair amount of wine. "It's because I love him." She cursed the shake in her voice. If Rafe knew she was crying, he'd think he'd won.

"It's late, Monique. For once, I think you are probably right, and we should talk about this when we've both had a good night's sleep. If you don't see that you have a problem as bad as Didi's, you are never going to get help. If you don't get help, I don't know how you'll survive alone."

"I don't need help." *And I'm not alone.*

"You do, but let's talk about it later. Get some sleep."

Monique heard something in Rafe's voice that scared her. "Wait, what is there to talk about? You can't expect me to sleep after saying we need to talk. If you have something to say, then say it now."

"I'm too tired to fight, Monique."

"Just say it, Rafe." She waited for the words, knowing he was going to end their relationship, hoping she was wrong.

"If you don't get some help and learn to trust people –

trust me – I don't think I can go on like this. I feel like I'm always proving myself to you. Like I keep sitting a test I can't pass."

Monique clenched her teeth, knowing that the first thing out of her mouth would be the worst thing she could say. If she said they should end it, she'd just prove Rafe's point. And that might really be the end of the relationship. "You know I spoke to people after... after my dad did it."

"I know. And I know you think it didn't help, but you need to keep trying."

"Rafe, please don't make me do it again." The last time they'd prescribed drugs that made her feel only half-alive. It made her singing dull. Even with the drugs, she had jumped at every loud noise. No amount of help was able to get the stench of blood out of her skin. Time had done that, if not all of the stench, at least some.

"I can't keep doing what we're doing, Monique. I need you to give me something back."

"I think you were right. We're too tired to talk about this. I'm going to bed." She hung up before he could respond.

Pain in her hand made her look. Her fist was clenched so tight her fingernails had broken the skin. She relaxed her fingers, surprised at the effort it took. Rafe might have a point, but right now, it seemed like letting people into her life just added more problems, and more pain.

A few minutes later, Monique stared at the door to her apartment as though it was the only barrier between her and all the evil in the world. She was still trembling from the aftermath of her last visit to Alexi's apartment, and the two phone calls. There was no way she could venture back into the bloody scene of his murder, not yet. The urge to find answers lurked below the shock, forcing her to go back, but not yet. First, she needed to get control of her fears.

She leaned out through the window. It was still dark out, but the promise of dawn touched the edges of the world she could see. There was a feeling of coming light rather than that deep night blackness. She retrieved her cigarettes from the living room and leaned out into the chill. She wasn't sure why she bothered to go outside to smoke. It was only to keep Rafe happy and he wasn't going to come over. Regardless, it felt right to be outside with her cigarette. It had been so long since smoking inside felt normal.

The nicotine started doing its magic, her nerves calmed a little with every drag. Monique wondered if Rafe was right, did she push everyone so far away that they couldn't connect with her. Did she just take emotional support? Did she really not care about other people? The anger she felt at Didi and Rafe for telling her what might be the truth, showed she wasn't emotionally detached. She emptied her lungs of smoke at the thought that anger was probably not the best emotion to rely on.

Was that how her father had finally broken down? She tried to remember a time when he laughed, when he was tender with her mother. But she'd sifted through the memories so much with the psychologist that she no longer knew what was real, and what she'd made up to keep the woman happy.

Anyway, she felt more than anger. When she sang, she felt peace, maybe not an emotion, but at least not anger. And joy. When people loved her performance, she felt joy, or maybe happy. Was there a difference?

Flicking her cigarette butt out the window and into the gutter, Monique stared at the empty street. If she didn't care, why was she in so much pain? If Didi got clean would she be happy for the right reasons. Were there wrong reasons?

She lit a second cigarette, knowing it was going to make her feel a little sick along with the rush. Tomorrow she'd get some food in the house, because now she was starving and there was no place to get delivery.

Monique leaned against windowsill and looked down to study the sad shrubs underneath. Holly bushes were great for security. No burglar was going to brave a thorough scratching just to boost a stereo or TV. The thing is that's all the plants did. There was no joy in them, no color at this time of year. Was this how her life looked to others? Prickles and shades of black?

She took the last drag and went back into the living room, curling up under the throw and closing her eyes. Maybe an hour of sleep would help her get perspective. She'd argued with Rafe and Didi before, they had always found a way to forgive each other. What she didn't understand was this drive to solve the murder of a stranger. Even Snake was barely an acquaintance, so why couldn't she let the cops do their work? Even if they really suspected her, it wouldn't take much for a lawyer to get them to back off. She had a solid alibi for Alexi, and the fact that she'd called them about Snake should make them look harder for this Vincent guy.

It didn't make sense to her. The fact that she became almost catatonic at the sight of blood should be enough to keep her away, but the drive to find answers overcame the horror. Even when she had to crawl away from the apartment, something in her head was telling her she was missing a clue. That she'd have to go back. There, that was another emotion, curiosity. Monique wished Rafe were right, because if she didn't care, she wouldn't hurt.

Her thoughts slowed as sleep crept over her mind.

9

Monique jerked awake. The sun was shining through the window, and she heard people talking on the street, and a car door slam. The world was up and at its business and she'd slept for an hour or more. Untangling herself from her wrapping, she stretched out the stiffness of sleeping on a too short couch.

She brushed her teeth and decided to put her shower off until after she'd searched through Alexi's apartment. The memory of the blood turned her empty stomach. Breakfast could wait too. In fact, she'd clean up and go out for a full breakfast when she was done and get groceries. Her new life would start as soon as she satisfied this stupid urge to find a clue.

All she needed was the set of picks and an ounce or two of courage, and it would be over. As she put the toothpaste back into the drawer, she saw a jar of mentholated ointment. Hadn't she heard something about using that to cover up bad smells? Didi's voice came into her mind. Yes, he'd taken great pleasure in telling her all the gory details of some cop show. He'd been ten, and she'd been fifteen, long before either of them had to cover up their own gory history.

Monique smeared a dollop of the ointment on her upper lip. Breathing in deeply through her nose confirmed that she wouldn't smell anything other than menthol for a long time. All she had to worry about was what she would see, and that was easier to control.

She just needed the lock picks. They must be with her keys. She remembered putting them in the kitchen somewhere. Monique looked on the counter, no keys. She closed her eyes to try to force the memory of putting them down. Nothing came. She patted her pockets, even though she would have felt them digging in while she slept. Not there. Crap. She had been exhausted last night and this feeling of being rested wasn't going to last unless she showered and ate soon.

Turning to place her back against the door, Monique tried to retrace her steps from the time she staggered into her apartment. She moved through her home touching every surface, lifting every object until she got to the couch. Nothing flagged a memory of putting a handful of metal objects down.

She shook out the throw that had kept her warm. Still nothing. Pulling the cushions off, Monique saw her key ring sitting in the middle of the couch. Keys, but there were no picks stuffed between the cushions. Had she dropped them in the hall?

She rushed to open her door and scan the carpet. No picks. If she couldn't get into the apartment, Monique wasn't sure what she would do. Where did you buy lock picks? And did you need ID? Oh God, those were Didi's picks. If the cops found them, could they be traced back to him? If he was involved with this along with Snake, she'd just left evidence to link them.

A glance at Alexi's door in front of her flooded her mind with the memory of the panic from last night. She held onto her own door for support as the images ran like a movie.

She'd fled the apartment without locking the door. The lock was like hers, you needed to turn the knob on the inside before you closed it. The door wasn't locked. She didn't need the picks, but she did need to get them back before anyone else went in that apartment.

"Okay honey, I'll get the car. Be down in a minute," Mac's voice broke through her thoughts.

Before she could retreat behind her door, Mac opened his. "Hi, Monique, you look like crap. Did you hear about the Metal Head? I heard it was like something out of Kill Bill. Real Tarantino." He reached out to her. "Are you okay? I was just saying about looking like crap. You probably just need to sleep. You'll be your fine Vampira self if you get a good couple of hours in bed. I could help get you relaxed."

Monique laughed. He knew she wouldn't take him up on the offer. "Don't worry, Mac, I know I look like shit." She turned away. "I think you're right. I'm going back to bed."

"What's that on your lip?"

Monique wondered how much ointment she'd smeared. "I'm getting a cold. This should clear my chest so I can sing tonight."

Before he could say anything, his door opened, and a red-haired woman stepped out. She looked like she'd slept in her clothes, but Monique guessed that her clothes had lain on the floor while she'd slept with Mac.

"Hey. You said you were getting the car." Her voice was rough. "Who's this?"

"Sheila, this is my neighbor Monique. Monique, this is Sheila."

"My name is Shelly." She glared at Mac. "If you aren't going to get the car, call me a cab."

"No, come on, I'll take you home." Mac turned back to Monique, a sheepish look on his face. "I guess I'm getting old if I can't remember a name. Listen, I'll come into the club one of these days. It's been a while since I heard you sing."

"Let me know when you'll be there, and I'll make sure you

have a good table." Monique waved to Shelley and slipped into her apartment.

As soon as they left, she'd get herself across the hall. If she'd dropped the picks inside, the last thing she needed was the cops to show up and find them. Her fingerprints were all over them, and maybe Didi's. Dropping them had been stupid, no matter how panicked she was.

The stairwell door slammed, and Monique cracked hers open. As she was about to step out, one of the doors down the hall opened. She dodged back into her apartment, not interested in engaging everyone in a good morning chat. The stairwell door banged again. There was only one more apartment on the floor. Mrs. Dowd. She worked from home and Monique had never seen her up before noon.

She took a deep breath, feeling the rush of menthol clear her head, and dashed across the hall into the bloody crime scene. Leaning against the door when she closed it behind her, she realized that her hands were touching the wood. Monique jerked away and used her tee shirt to wipe, or at least smear, any fingerprints that might have stuck. She'd have to remember to wipe the knob outside before she left.

Breaking and entering was more complicated than it had seemed when she first thought about it.

This time she didn't turn on a light, there was enough sunlight shining through the cracks in the blinds to let her see to search without highlighting the mess in the middle of the room. Maybe she could pretend it didn't exist. The menthol was working. It was all she could smell. The picks were lying in the middle of the carpet. She scooped them up and slid them into a pocket. The bedroom seemed the best bet. If he'd kept the bag in there, maybe that's where he'd kept all his valuables. And if she started in the bedroom, she would be moving toward the front door, and escape, as she searched the rest of the apartment. It might help her push aside any reactions, knowing she was on her way out of the apartment all the time.

She had no idea what she was looking for. Perhaps a clue as to what might have been in the bag, maybe the identity of this mysterious man who scared Snake so much. She tiptoed around the edge of the room, careful not to touch anything this time, and stepped into the bedroom.

How much searching had Vincent done? If he'd been interested only in the bag, or its contents, he might have missed something. She looked at the mess and decided to start with the closet because she hadn't looked there earlier. Wrapping her tee shirt around her hand to protect the knob from prints, she pulled the bi-fold doors open.

There were a couple of shirts on wire hangers, and a leather jacket, but nothing else seemed to be disturbed. So, maybe, Vincent had stopped when he'd found what he was looking for. It didn't help her understand what she was hoping to find, but it gave her some hope that she wasn't wasting her time. She felt the shirts to see if anything was tucked up a sleeve, then moved to the leather jacket. As she reached for the pocket, she realized the leather might hold a print. Her tee shirt wouldn't work for gloves unless she slipped it off, and she wasn't willing to do that just in case the police came back. There was no way they'd finished with the apartment as a crime scene, no matter how many murders they had on the list.

Pulling one of the shirts off the hanger, Monique buttoned the cuffs, and then slipped her arms into the sleeves with the body hanging in front of her. Folding the cuffs to keep her hands from slipping out, she carefully patted the front pockets of the jacket before reaching inside. A transit pass and five quarters were the only contents. She returned them. There were two inside pockets, but neither yielded any clues.

Keeping the shirt as her gloves, Monique looked under the

bed, only dust bunnies. And no holes in the bottom of the box spring that might hide a file folder or something interesting. She pushed herself up and went to the mattress. The side facing her was whole, if stained and grubby. She lifted the corner nearest her trying not to let it fall. The cops would probably notice if the mattress was flopped onto the floor.

There was nothing hidden in the mattress, so she moved on to the dresser. The drawers were all on the floor, broken. Unless Alexi had microchips stuck to them, there was no clue there. The frame of the dresser was clean. Monique tipped it forward, and something crackled. Pulling it farther away from the wall, she saw an envelope attached to the back with tape. Carefully grasping the edge with the shirt still on her hands, Monique pulled it free. It didn't contain much, but she slid it into her pocket and pushed the dresser back against the wall.

There was nothing left to do, and now that she wasn't searching, she felt the shakes starting in her gut and chest. Monique shed the shirt and hung it on one of the empty hangers. She stood for a moment gathering herself for the walk through the living room.

She opened the door to the bedroom and checked the living room in case anything else looked like it was a good hiding place for clues, forcing her eyes to track the whole room, even the, now dried, blood in the center. To ease the tension, she could feel building she used an old technique she'd learned from the counselor, about the only useful thing she got from her. Wiggling the fingers of her free hand. It was supposed to give her mind something to do so it didn't focus on the problem. It worked a little. At least she didn't feel like running from the room screaming.

Vincent had tossed the place. If he'd killed Alexi, why had he come back for the bag? Perhaps he was worried about over-staying his welcome the first time. She could relate to that. She was starting to feel the need to leave. Nothing jumped out at her as a good hiding place – at least nothing that wasn't already tossed.

Monique patted her pocket to make sure the picks hadn't fallen out again. She started around the edge of the room. Keeping her hands tucked tight to her side. There was only the doorknob to clean, and lock, then she'd be done with this. As she slipped past the bathroom, the memory of searching the kitchen and bathroom sucked the heat from her body.

She still had to wipe away any traces of her fingers, or DNA, on anything she'd touched, or might have touched. Would that leave the cops with nothing to find? Not even Alexi's prints? That would definitely set off alarms. But it was better than trying to explain what she'd been doing in here after she'd said they had barely noticed each other. Her tee shirt wasn't going to be enough. Monique was going to need to get something from her cleaning supplies. A cloth she could throw away. One more trip across the hall, this time she would leave her own keys and the picks in her place. Without them, there would be nothing to lose, nothing to slow her down.

A dash across the hall and back took less than a minute. She was grateful there were only a few apartments. She reminded herself that everyone was out – or was unlikely to be leaving their apartment, so she would have time to do what she needed to do. As she opened Alexi's door, she heard a phone ringing. The sound so unexpected, she froze with her hand on the lock. The ring cut out and she heard Alexi's voice ask the caller to leave a message, definitely eastern European. It was weirdly old fashioned for Alexi to have an answering machine.

"Alexi, where are you? We need to talk. The Colonel thinks you stole something. If you don't call me, I can't protect you. If he kills you, I will find another way to collect on your debt. You have a sister, yes?"

The message ended.

Monique blew out a breath. She'd been worried that the cops would return and catch her, what if this guy showed up, or sent someone? Would he have the mystery man with him? Was this colonel the mystery man?

She dashed into the bathroom and thought about what she'd touched. Thank god, it was so filthy, she'd only touched the medicine cabinet handle, afraid of getting anything on her hands. After wiping it clean, she returned to the kitchen. Now she was glad he kept his home dirty. It meant she'd minimized what she let touch her skin. Had she come in contact with anything other than drawer handles and cupboard pulls? Had she leaned against the counter? No, she remembered flinching away from the stained laminate. It only took seconds to wipe the handles and then she was done.

Monique went to the door, pushed in the lock, and wiped the handle. She leaned close to the door and listened, her fingers twitching again to release some of the built up tension. No sounds came from the hall. As she turned the doorknob, she froze.

Light switches. The first time in, she'd turned on the light in the hall and bedroom. Swearing under her breath, she skirted through the apartment, wiped the light switch in the bedroom, ran back, and rubbed at the hall switch. Ripping open the door, Monique stepped into the corridor, closed the door, tested the lock, and then almost dove into her own apartment. Never again, no matter how much she felt the need, she would never go through that again.

10

Monique kept moving, not wanting to experience the consequences of the shock. She hoped the constant activity would help until it passed, although it never had before. A shower, a change of clothes, breakfast, and then she'd figure out what was in the envelope. Maybe it was something she could give to the cops, to help them solve the murders. There was no doubt that Snake and Alexi were killed, if not by the same person, for the same reason. She knew in her gut that this Colonel guy was behind it, whatever the hell it happened to be.

She grabbed a garbage bag and threw the gloves and cleaning cloth inside. She stripped and threw her clothes in. Another outfit she would never wear again. She started the shower and waited until the water was steaming before stepping in. Two minutes later, she was toweling herself dry, skin red from the heat.

Keep moving.

She knew if she could do that, the panic she could feel pushing at her nerves wouldn't take control. Monique scrubbed at her hair, trying to dry it. Then she ran for clothes, stumbling over the edge of the rug in her bedroom. As she fell, Monique curled into a ball, the realization she couldn't outrun the panic dropped on her. Naked and cold, lying on the carpet, she stopped fighting and let it flow over her. It started with shakes, and then gasping sobs, then she was gulping for air as the world went black around her.

She woke up shivering. This time it was just from the cold. The panic had gone, leaving her feeling empty. Her hair was still wet, so she knew it hadn't been long. Monique pulled herself up to sit on the edge of her bed. Her left arm and leg were dusted with fluff from the rug, but there was no other damage.

The hollow feeling inside wasn't just hunger. It was as if all the horror was cried out of her soul. She knew it wasn't permanent, but at least she was able to start moving again. It felt like someone had erased everything from her life, and she could choose what came back in. It was a good feeling, even if it was a delusion.

She rubbed her skin to remove the fluff and then dried her hair. When she was dressed, Monique gathered all the trash in her apartment and stuffed the garbage bag full. The envelope went into her purse and she grabbed a jacket. She was starving, and if crying was so cleansing then food might give her the energy she needed for the next steps.

When Monique opened her door, she came to a stop. In front of Alexi's apartment, his back to her, was a man, stocky and head shaved to stubble. He was listening at the door. Was this the Colonel? Fear froze her from stomach to head.

There was no way for her to avoid being noticed. If she retreated to the apartment, it might signal that she knew something, so she pulled her door closed and turned to lock it as though there was nothing wrong. She sensed the man turn around as she finished.

He stared at her. What was it with Alexi's visitors and the

creepy expressions? Gray eyes, a scar running from his right eyebrow to his cheek, twisting his face into a grimace. He tried a smile and said, "Good morning. Do you know, Alexi? Your neighbor?" He was obviously trying to sound pleasant. The effect was just weird, like that doll in the horror movies, Chucky. His voice also brought back memories of her search. It was the man on the phone.

"No, he's new." She turned to walk away.

He took a step toward her. "Do you know where he is?"

"No," she said, then decided that it might send him away if she told him the truth. "Well, he's dead, so..."

The forced smile turned into a scowl. "Dead? When?"

"Yesterday. You should talk to the police. They were here asking questions." Monique turned to leave. She expected him to ask something else, or to say something else. When he pushed roughly past her and stormed through the stairwell door, she felt relief.

Monique waited until he had time to clear the building. The thought of being in the stairwell with him almost made her consider taking the highly unreliable elevator.

SHE TOOK a table in the back of Mitch's Diner. There weren't that many people in, but it was getting close to morning coffee time, and she didn't want anyone who was standing in line for a coffee and donut to be looking over her shoulder.

"Hey, Monique, it's been a while. What's your pleasure?" Jack was waiter, prep cook, busboy, and owner of the cafe.

"Hey, Jack. I'm starving, bacon, eggs, pancakes, and coffee."

"Everything cooked the usual way? And sourdough toast?"

She nodded and pulled out the envelope as soon as Jack turned away. Inside was a picture. One man staring off into the distance. He was tall, face ruddy, gray hair bushy with a trimmed goatee. It had been cropped badly. It looked like the picture was taken from a larger shot. Someone's shoulder jutted into the corner of the frame.

"Still, black?" Jack's voice cut through her thoughts, confusing her until she saw the coffee cup in his hand.

"Yeah. I don't see that changing soon, thanks, Jack." She stared at the picture while she waited for breakfast. He didn't look familiar. He looked like someone in charge, someone you'd call for help. Maybe it was the way he was focused on something in the distance, as if he saw more than the common person did.

Jack slid her plate in front of her and went back to the kitchen. Monique placed the picture on the table so she could look at it while she ate. The flavor of bacon reminded her how hungry she was, so she took her attention off the picture until she'd eaten half the food on her plate and had to slow down so she could digest.

The photo was set in a village. It looked like an Italian one, although Monique was pretty sure lots of countries had villages with stone walls and shuttered houses. So this was important enough to Alexi to hide it, which meant he might be planning to use it. And this was what the Colonel had killed for, or at least part of why. She just needed to figure out why it was important, and then give it to the cops. Well, she also had to figure out a way to explain how she came into possession of it, and why she didn't just hand it over first thing.

She took her phone out and tapped the Google icon. There must be something that could help her identify this guy, or the town, or something that could help her get to the next step. A quick search gave her an app called Google Goggles. She downloaded the app and let it install as she finished the last bites of her pancakes. Pushing her plate across the table so Jack could clear without disturbing her, Monique played with the app until she understood how to use it.

"Still hungry?" Jack asked, filling her cup and lifting the plate.

Monique laughed. "Not right now, but I've missed a few meals. I can't guarantee I won't need a burger in five minutes."

"You need some more meat on you, girl. You keep doing whatever you are doing. I'll keep the coffee coming." Jack was always good about letting her hangout even when it got busy. Monique knew that she had the table as long as she needed it.

She returned to the app. It would try to identify anything in a picture she took with her phone. Monique smoothed the photo and took a picture of the man – no magic answer. She waited a few minutes hoping for something, but nothing happened. She decided she might have done it wrong. Looking around she saw a newspaper in the booth across from her. Grabbing it, she flipped through, looking for a photo of someone she recognized. The entertainment page had full sized shots of the new James Bond.

Monique took a picture, and within seconds the app returned a result, Daniel Craig. Okay so she was using it right, maybe this guy was camera shy. She took a picture of the street he was standing in, as much as she could get into one shot. The app returned the name Konjic, Bosnia. She tapped the Google search bar again and typed, The Colonel, Bosnia. The first link that returned was to *The Times*, a UK link. The headline read *Javor Dragic, aka The Colonel, remains a fugitive*. She followed the link to learn that the man was a Serbian War criminal.

There was a picture, kind of like a mug shot. The man had dead eyes, black like Vincent's. His face was square, and the goatee made him look like a devil. She barely recognized him. She could see how the app had missed the connection. She wouldn't have thought they were the same man. Now all she needed to do was figure out who the hell he was pretending to be in Vancouver.

·   ·   ·

AN HOUR LATER, Monique sat on her couch at home. It was almost lunchtime. Didi would be going through his treatment by now. She didn't expect him to call when he was done. He'd remember they were fighting and continue to punish her for a few hours. She dialed the number for his friend Andy. The call went to voice mail.

"Andy, I don't know what Didi told you, but I hope you can let me know what's going on with him." She left her phone number.

Monique itched to get into action. She couldn't think of how to find this Colonel without talking to someone who knew Alexi, or maybe Snake. She wasn't stupid enough to ask Vincent, even if she could find him. She couldn't help picturing the dead eyes staring at her. Given what she'd overheard on the phone, she couldn't ask the guy who was at Alexi's this morning, or anyone else who came to the door.

She considered telling the police what she knew, but the same two things held her back. She had no legal right to have broken into the apartment, and that action might put her back on the suspect list. And she was pretty sure the information she had wasn't enough to help them do anything.

She'd run out of ideas on how to find someone who wanted to stay hidden. As sure as she was that this Javor Dragic was in Vancouver, she was certain that he wouldn't be using that name.

It was too quiet in the apartment. She needed people around her, and she needed to talk even if no one had information for her. She gathered her things and headed to the club. There she could relax and enjoy the other musicians, maybe join someone on stage for a set. She'd done this so many times before and it had seemed normal, this time it felt more like seeking refuge than company. Then again, her days hadn't been that much different before this. Being around murder seemed to heighten her senses.

Maybe fighting with everyone she cared about did that too.

It was quiet in the club. Afternoons were sometimes like that. Tess was running an open mike, looking for a few new house singers now that the city let the clubs stay open so much later. Tess turned as Monique entered. She waved her over. "Come help me choose."

Monique noticed four other women sitting at the bar. "How many have you auditioned so far?"

"This is number two. The first one couldn't carry a tune in a bucket." Tess went to the bar and grabbed a glass. "Here, on me."

Monique sniffed the glass, a nice Cabernet. She nodded to the girl on stage who couldn't have been more than eighteen. "What are you going to sing?"

"Night and Day."

Monique shook her head. "That's not going to showcase your voice. I'll give you some advice. Try doing something from a different playlist and make it your kind of jazz."

The girl frowned for a second, and then brightened. "Okay, how about *Oh! Darling.* My mom used to sing it to me."

Monique checked with Ray who was playing for the auditions, he nodded back and ran the first few phrases before saying, "When you're ready."

While the girl sang, Tess leaned in. "That was good advice."

"I learned it early on. No one is really looking for the same old thing. They want something fresh. Anyway, she's good."

Tess sipped her own wine before speaking. Monique could almost see the wheels turning. "Yeah, she needs some maturing. Would you help her?"

Monique considered. Was she willing to spend time mentoring another singer? The real question was what else would she do? "Sure, why not. How many are you planning on taking?"

"Two. You don't need to worry; I'm not cutting back on your gigs." Tess waved at the girl. "What's your name, child?"

"Maisie. I go by Maisie Lee."

"Okay, you go sit down there. Next girl up."

They went through the other four women who'd been paying attention because they sang everything but jazz. One of them, Laura, made the cut. Monique gave advice to the other three. Their voices were more suited to rock and gospel, and she knew they would have more luck sticking to their strengths.

She waited while Tess gave instructions to Laura and Maisie. They left, Ray went to the lounge, and Tess brought coffee to the table. "One glass of wine at this time of day is enough. Now, it looks to me like you want to talk about something?"

How much could she tell Tess? It was hard to know where her boss's priorities lay. Monique considered what might make Tess help without getting her suspicions up. Tess was pretty connected, not because she was crooked, but because she didn't much care what people did as long as they kept it out of the club.

Maybe she had some information that would lead Monique to the Colonel. Not that she'd go after him. When she could point the police to something concrete – like proof of a war criminal living in their town – she would. "You know anything about a group of Serbs living here?"

Tess narrowed her eyes. "What are you getting into?"

Monique was surprised by the question. Tess seemed to care about her, not just the bottom line. Although maybe Tess cared about the customers Monique brought to the club. "Nothing, but I can't get this murder off my mind. I don't like what's happening. All I know is that there's some connection between my neighbor and Snake. The cops don't seem to be doing anything other than questioning me."

"You stay away from these Serbian guys. I don't want to hire another singer when they kill you. And how will Maisie get any better without your help?"

She started to say, 'I can take care of myself', but realized it would shut Tess down, and that would bring an end to any information she would be willing to share. "I'm not sure staying away is possible, Tess. They killed that guy across the hall from me, and Snake down the lane. I'll be careful, I promise. Will you tell me what you know?"

Tess stirred her coffee, thinking it over. Monique watched the decision get made as Tess firmed her lips. Looking Monique in the eye, she started talking, "Most of the people who came here were looking for a place to settle peacefully. Some of them were looking to expand their operations, and some are here to hide. It's the same with any people. I guess you're asking about the last two types?"

"Yes, I think so. How do you know this?"

"I know about people. I came here from somewhere. I know about settling into a new world. And I know how it works when it's about money and power. I know how bad it can get. I just don't know any of the people you need to talk to."

Monique finished her coffee, not sure she believed Tess, but knowing better than to push. "Thanks anyway, boss."

11

An hour later, the club started to fill with the early evening crowd. People who were willing to sit and drink until the entertainment started or were there for the drinks not the jazz. Monique had switched to water when the coffee pot was empty. Now she sat at the bar and watched the activity as people wandered in.

One of those people was a friend of Snake's. Monique watched her slide into a booth and order a drink, something long and dark. Her name was something like Celia... Celie... Celeste, yes. Monique wondered at the fact that the only reason she knew these people was because of Didi's life. He had some sleazy friends, but they were coming in handy right now. And at least he had friends. She didn't have many. She didn't know which of them had a better life.

She watched Celeste swallow half the drink in one gulp. The girl didn't look well. She was shorter than Monique was, maybe four foot nine, but even at nineteen her body was padded at hips and bust in a way Monique's was never going to be. If Celeste was drinking that fast, there was probably something going on. Maybe she'd know who Snake was – had been – involved with.

Monique ordered another of whatever Celeste was drinking and took it with her to the booth.

"It's been a while since I saw you last, Celeste. How are you doing?" Monique slid into the booth, staying close to the edge, so she couldn't be trapped if someone else joined them. "You waiting for someone?"

Celeste finished her glass and then pulled the second one to her, taking a smaller sip. "No, just wanted to see what's going on." Her eyes wandered to the door. "You seen Snake?"

Monique didn't want to be the one to tell her what happened. There was no way to make that kind of news easy to swallow. No matter what kind of life you lived. "When did you last see him?"

"A couple days ago. He said he'd be here, so I thought I'd check it out. You still singing here?"

Nodding, Monique sipped her own drink. "What is Snake into these days?"

"Credit cards. You know, it's big business. No one gets hurt except the big credit card companies and they make too much money anyway. But you won't tell anyone, right?"

Nice justification. Monique had learned that justification was often the only difference between a thief and a law-abiding citizen. She settled against the backrest, unwilling to push, or end the conversation. "I hear some rough characters get into that."

"Yeah, but it's good money. Didi was thinking of getting into it. I haven't seen him either." Celeste was getting twitchy, her gaze roaming the room and flashing back to the door whenever someone came through.

"Didi's getting clean," Monique said, hoping it was true.

Celeste finished her drink and slid around the bench to leave. "Good luck to him. Drugs are a crap way to live your life, right? Look, if Snake comes around let him know I was looking for him, okay?"

Monique couldn't let Celeste go without telling her about Snake. It was going to hurt the girl, but it would hurt no matter when she learned the truth. "Celeste, I should have told you this already, but Snake is dead. He was killed last night. I'm sorry."

The girl slumped, her hands rubbing at her face. Monique saw tears slip through the gap between her fingers. "I knew he was getting in too deep. I told him to stop." She straightened and wiped her face with her sleeve. "I guess it was inevitable. Any idea who did it?" She picked up her glass and looked for more drink in the bottom.

Monique knew enough about grief to know Celeste was denying her feelings by trying to be cool. They'd hit hard soon. But then maybe Celeste knew that, and just wanted to be alone when she broke down. "A guy named Vincent."

Celeste rattled the ice, clearly hinting that Monique owed her a drink. Monique didn't bite.

Shrugging, Celeste answered, "Never heard of him."

"Do you know who Snake was working for?" Monique wanted to comfort the girl, but didn't know how, and Celeste seemed to have taken control of herself.

"He wouldn't tell me. I guess he wanted to protect me." She jumped out of her seat. "I gotta go. Tell Didi I hope he gets straight. I'm out of here. I'm going home to Manitoba. I can't deal with this shit." She hurried out of the club.

Monique felt like crap, as if she had driven Celeste away. She knew it wasn't her fault that Snake had stepped over the line. But her relief that Didi hadn't jumped on this job with Snake was tainted with regret for the dead man.

She was still stuck. She had no idea what her next step in finding the Colonel was.

Didi hadn't called her, and neither had Andy. Tess was somewhere out of the club. Everyone had something better to do with their time than stumble around guessing about war criminals and murderers.

She didn't feel like singing, so no reason to stay sober. Leaving the booth, she went to sit at the bar again. Tess hated it when seating for two was taken by one person. Hitching herself on the last stool at the far side of the bar, Monique ordered a shot of *Don Patron* and sat back to enjoy the show.

Two shots later, Monique suddenly had a reason to stay sober. Vincent had come into the club. He looked around and then joined the other sole patrons at the bar. He took the last stool at the other end from Monique and ordered a beer. From where he sat, he could see the stage, but Monique was out of his line of sight.

She watched him as he scanned the room. He must have been waiting for someone. He didn't seem too worried that the person was late. Monique wondered if Vincent was waiting for the Colonel. Perhaps she'd get lucky and be able to hand this over to the police tonight. Or were war criminals the RCMP's jurisdiction? No matter, she had Detective Adams' phone number and the cops could sort out the jurisdiction.

"Do you want anything else, Monique?" Todd, tonight's bartender, interrupted her train of thought.

"No, just put the shots on my tab, and I'll stick with water for the rest of the night, thanks." There was no way she was going to muddy her brain at this point. This Vincent guy was dangerous, but she was going to keep an eye on him, no matter what happened.

Vincent finished his beer and threw a bill on the bar. Monique grabbed her purse, reached in, and turned her phone to silent, so she didn't have to worry it about ringing and giving her away when she followed him. He didn't move. Monique felt like she was holding her breath. Had Vincent come for the singers? Had this become the place for criminals to hang out?

She'd have to let Tess know who was coming in, so she could put an end to it.

Vincent checked his watch and stood.

Monique stayed where she was.

He turned to leave and made it through the, now crowded, entrance before she moved. Knowing how quickly she'd lost him last time, she wanted to be close enough to follow, but not so close that he would notice she was there.

When Monique got through the door, she saw Vincent crossing the intersection and heading downhill. Unless he was headed to a parked car, he was going downtown. It was only a dozen or so blocks from The Blue Scene to the Downtown Eastside. That was the perfect place for a war criminal to hide out, as long as he didn't want a luxurious lifestyle. Monique bent to light a cigarette then slowly followed Vincent.

Monique talked herself off the edge of panic. She was just another person walking while she smoked. Nothing of interest here. She kept her gaze aimed at the wet sidewalk a few feet in front of her, just like anyone who was out for a walk at night. Every few steps she flicked her glance up to make sure Vincent was still there.

After a few blocks, Vincent turned into a side street. Monique hurried to catch up. If he entered one of the old buildings, she'd never figure out which one. Too many of them were business offices, or lofts above stores, so few of them had lighted showrooms that would display the people inside. None of them would be likely to have an unlocked door if she had to step off the street.

She turned the corner and saw him. She also saw that the street ended only two blocks in from Main. And there was only one building that might be apartments, where she could pretend to be visiting someone.

Monique went cold. She was about to be caught. Wherever Vincent went, he'd see she wasn't going anywhere legitimate. He'd know she was following. And she realized it was going to look even more suspicious if she turned on her heel and left the street. The only thing she could do was brave it out and hope to survive.

Vincent stopped beside a black Audi before turning and looking right at her. Monique ignored his dead eyes and kept walking. She told herself that's what women did when they were on a street at night and a strange man looked at them. Her heart was working so hard she expected it to rattle her body.

She was getting closer to Vincent, and the end of the street was only a half block away. There was light coming from the lobby of the last building. Maybe there was a party. She just kept walking; eyes focused straight ahead.

She saw Vincent reach for the door handle and slide into the driver's seat. The engine purred and the headlights came on. He pulled the car away from the curb and drove out to Main Street.

Monique slowed and bent to light another cigarette to hide the fact she was looking at the license plate. It was partially obscured, but she got one of the letters and all three numbers: A731. That was something she could give to the cops, and not have to worry about explaining herself. They would find the car, and if not The Colonel, at least Vincent could be taken off the street. Maybe there would be time to let Celeste know Snake's killer had been arrested before she went back east.

Monique reached the end of the street. There was a party going on in the last building. She looked over her shoulder and saw that Vincent had gone. Relieved because she wasn't in the party mood, Monique turned back toward the lights of Main Street. She just wanted to get home and call the cops. And call Andy again to find out if Didi was done. If he was clean. To think about what her brother would need from her to stay clean. How she would keep him in her life despite what Rafe predicted.

12

Monique tossed her keys on the kitchen counter and continued to the living room, opening the window and leaning out. The walk home had been fast, and she'd felt eyes on her back the entire way. Now she was in her apartment, a sense of safety folded over her. Maybe it was false safely, but it was comforting. At least now, she could make the calls without feeling like she was being watched. She lit a cigarette and pulled her phone out of her pocket.

Looking at the back of the card Detective Adams had given her, Monique saw three numbers, a direct line, cell phone, and emergency. It wasn't exactly an emergency. She dialed the direct line, hoping that meant someone would pick up even if Detective Adams wasn't there.

"Detective Watson."

She held the phone out and checked the number she'd dialed. "I thought this was Detective Adams' number." She didn't want to talk to Watson. He was too good at getting her guard down.

"Yeah. He's not here right now. Who is this?"

She pushed aside her dislike for the man, knowing he would

be following up anyway. "Monique Duchesne. I saw the guy who killed Snake tonight."

"Where? I hope you haven't gone looking for him. Ms. Duchesne, this man is dangerous. Please stay away from this case."

Monique smiled. If only life were that simple.

If she could be sure the cops were going to investigate, if she knew Didi had no connection, or if the case didn't keep coming at her, she would happily stay away. "I'll do my best. I have a license plate, at least most of it." She gave him the information.

"I'll see if we can get an identification from that, but I doubt he used a car that was registered to him. Is there anything else?"

Monique couldn't think of a legitimate way to explain her knowledge that a Serbian war criminal was involved. *Yes, I broke into your crime scene and found evidence that I didn't call you about,* didn't seem like the smartest thing to say. "No, that's all."

"Okay, we'll follow up. Stay away from this, Ms. Duchesne. I would hate to be looking for your killer too."

Monique said she would and hung up. Somehow, his assurance they would follow up didn't make her feel better.

She ignored the little voice that told her the call had been a waste of time and leaned against the windowsill before dialing Andy's number. Maybe there would be some good news about Didi. It had been almost a whole day.

"Hello?"

"Andy?"

"Yeah, who's this?"

"Didi's sister. I was hoping for an update on his progress." She held her breath, sure that the news wouldn't be good. That Didi had bailed.

"He's still under, Monique. They delayed the start. He'll be under for another two or three hours."

"So there will be news around one? You can call me. I'll be awake."

Andy didn't respond. The pause went on long enough that Monique spoke again, "You can call me, even if Didi is still mad at me. The addiction caused the fight. It's happened before. I know I should have given him a break, but..."

"I know, Monique. It's not that. Even without the drugs, you and Didi were always fighting and then getting over it right away. That seems to be how you love each other. It's just that I don't know what Didi told you about this treatment."

Monique took a breath. "I know it's just going to get rid of the drugs in his system. We'll have to work on the addiction."

"Yeah, that's true. Well, true enough, Didi will have to work on the addiction, Monique. You need to let him do it."

"He'll need my help." She wasn't going to let Didi do this alone, no matter what Andy said.

"Yes, you can help him. You can support him. That's not the problem. You need to let him take control of the process. You need to let him grow up."

"I don't know if he can..."

"Maybe you should let him try."

"Maybe," Monique said. If she didn't argue with Andy, he couldn't keep pushing on this.

Andy sighed. "Fine, we'll talk about it later. Since you didn't mention it, I guess Didi didn't tell you about the potential downside."

Trust Didi to leave out any problems. Looking at only what he wanted to see had been his trouble all his life. "No, I guess I should have looked it up. How bad could it get?"

"Most of the time it works fine. The problem is Didi won't feel the withdrawal because he's under anesthetic, but his body will. He's been an addict a long time. His body isn't in great shape. We think he'll be okay, but I might be calling with bad news."

Monique's stomach contracted. Didi was all the family she

had. The drugs had been bad enough, but she'd never considered he'd die. She realized how naive that had been. Addicts died all the time, if not from overdoses, from bad heroin. "Let's hope not. I want the call anyway. I need to know. Please, tell me you'll call."

"Okay, I promise. I'll call even if he tells me not to. He'll be weak, but maybe you can visit him tomorrow."

"Where's he staying afterward? He can come here if he needs to."

"He's staying with me. I'll take care of him, Monique. I want him clean too."

Monique wondered how many other friends Didi had kept up with from their past. She'd slipped away from that world, tired of the sympathetic looks, and feeling like she had to prove she wouldn't just lash out and kill someone. "Thanks, Andy. I don't know why Didi deserves this, but thanks."

"Monique, I thought you knew. Um, Didi and I, we're together. We're a couple."

Tears formed in her eyes, not sure if they were about being happy that Didi had found someone who cared that much, or jealousy that her brother was emotionally healthier than she was, despite the addiction. She blinked away the tears and swallowed to loosen her throat. "I'm glad. Thanks for telling me. I have to go, Andy. Please call me either way."

"I will. You take care."

MONIQUE CRAWLED INTO BED. After the call from Andy, she told herself to let everyone else take care of things. Her exhaustion drew her into sleep until almost noon. There was no message from Andy when she woke, but she didn't worry. She told herself that Didi was safe with him.

She filled her day with cleaning and grocery shopping. As

she did Didi's laundry, it occurred to her that it was weird that he'd dropped this off with her. That he didn't leave it with Andy. Then again, with what he'd told her about how low he'd sunk, it made all kinds of Didi sense.

Eventually bored with housework, and not feeling like cooking even though she'd filled her fridge and cupboards, she went to the club to warm up her voice. She'd eat later. Singing on a full stomach didn't always work anyway.

She chatted with Ray and Wes, until it was time to go on stage. "Why don't we have some fun with it tonight? Let's start with that new version of *Over the Rainbow,* and then you can surprise me with the rest."

"Girl, we can play stump the band if you want. Tess loves it when we get the audience involved," Ray said.

Monique laughed, amazed at the difference between her feelings yesterday and today. Handing over her problems to the police had lifted a weight from her.

The set went well, the audience managed to stump Ray and Monique twice which always made for a great night. The new girl, Maisie, was getting her shot with a set right after theirs. Ray and the guys stayed on stage to accompany her. Monique took a glass of soda water to the lounge with her and decided not to have a smoke. If Didi could kick his habit, she'd try to give up cigarettes. She wasn't looking forward to her own withdrawal symptoms, but it would have to happen eventually, it might as well be now.

Barry walked in behind her. "Monique, there's a call for you." He handed her the handset for the club phone. It was unusual, but not rare, for artists to get calls to the club. Fans wanted to talk to their favorites occasionally, and no one gave out their personal contact information to potentially crazy fans.

"Hello?" Monique lowered herself into the couch.

"You are the singer?" Monique froze, barely able to breath. It was a man, unfamiliar voice, but he had an Eastern European accent. Vincent? The Colonel?

She didn't answer. Mostly because she couldn't force any air through her lungs.

"I take that as yes. I have for you a warning. Stay away from things you don't understand."

"Who is this?" Monique hated the quaver in her voice.

"You don't know me. If you did, you would be dead soon."

"That doesn't make any sense. Why did you call me.?"

"Someone tells me you are asking questions. These are answers you do not want. Go back to singing. Your voice is very good. It would be a pity to lose it, yes?"

Monique ended the call. He was trying to scare her off, and it had worked. There was no need to listen to any more. She wanted to throw up, run home, call the police, or faint. She couldn't do any of that.

Screw quitting. She pulled her cigarettes out and reached into the drawer where Ali kept a bottle of cheap whiskey. He'd forgive her, and she'd replace it. Pouring a good shot into her soda water Monique headed for the back alley.

When she got there, she told herself not to think about Snake getting killed. It had to be okay for her to come out and smoke – at least until she could quit. She lit up and took a deep drag, the nicotine flooding her with a zing of pleasure before it calmed her enough that she could figure out what to do.

Regardless of whether it was the Colonel, or Vincent, or someone else, she was busted. She had to tell the police. She had to stop investigating on her own. As she thought about leaving the investigation to the police, a flash of memory stopped her. Snake, gasping out his last breath in her presence. Her mother doing the same thing.

The fear ebbed leaving a growing heat of fury in her heart.

There was no way she could trust that she would be safe if

she stopped searching for the killer. If she let the cops take care of it, she would never know when the next death would happen, never know if she was safe. The fact that someone had called her, said she wasn't safe now. And just because he hadn't threatened anyone but her, didn't mean that Didi wouldn't be a target if they found out about him.

Monique lit a second cigarette with the stub of her first, throwing the finished one into a puddle, and hearing a satisfying hiss as it was extinguished. The glass in her hand was losing its ice. She swallowed half the contents between drags on the cigarette. The combination of nicotine and alcohol made her dizzy at first. When that faded, she was left with a clarity that shoved away all the worries.

All she needed to think about right now was her next set. She looked at the cigarette in her fingers, damn, now she'd have to warm up again after the smokefest. Why didn't she think about that first? When she was done for the night, she'd call Detective Adams, or Watson, whoever answered the phone. She'd tell them about the threat. Then she'd figure out how to find The Colonel before he could do any more damage.

Pulling the door wide behind her, she heard Maisie start signing *Someone to Watch Over Me*, her last song. Monique would need to be on stage in ten minutes. She flicked her half-smoked cigarette into the puddle and ran back into the lounge to start warming up. Ray would expect her to pick all the songs for the next set. In normal circumstances, she'd have no problem winging it. Tonight it was hard to think about one new song, let alone ten.

"Great set, Monique. It's been a while since I played some of those oldies." Wes patted her shoulder as they filed into the lounge.

Monique had dug deep into her memory and found some standards by Nina Simone that matched her mood. Sprinkling in a little Sarah Vaughn had softened it enough for the audience. And she knew Maisie wouldn't have chosen any of them because few people sang the real oldies these days. Monique didn't want to step on the girl's toes while she was still learning.

"I'm done," Wes continued. "You want to join us for a late night burger at Maria's?"

Monique shook her head. "I'll stay for a drink and then I'm heading home." The fewer people she hung around with, the fewer targets for Vincent and his minions. She'd call the cops as soon as the guys left and get them to meet her at home.

Two minutes later, she was alone in the lounge. As she pulled out her cell phone, a flash of panic went through her nerves. Was she doing the right thing? Was she being stupid? Her only answer was yes, to both things. It wasn't always smart to do the right thing. If she just folded, she'd be looking over her shoulder forever. And more people would die, or get pulled into whatever The Colonel and Vincent were involved in. And she suspected that whatever they were doing now would just get worse the longer they got away with it.

Although what could be worse than acts that got you labeled as a war criminal?

She scrolled through her call history and pressed redial on the call to Detective Adams. It rang three times.

"Monique, the cops are here to see you," Tess said as she walked through the door.

Clicking the phone shut, Monique looked up. Detective Watson walked through the door, Adams behind him. "Thanks, Tess. It's fine." She waited until Tess left and then said, "I was just calling you."

"You have something to tell us?" Watson's voice was hard, and he stared at her as though he could pin her to the chair.

Monique stopped herself from responding to the tone. She needed them to be on her side. "Yes, I got a call tonight. I was threatened."

"Is that all?" Watson didn't seem interested.

"I don't know who he was, but his accent made me think of that Vincent guy."

"Why would you get a call like that, Ms. Duchesne?" Now Adams was back to playing good cop to Watson's bad cop.

Monique sucked her lips in while she thought about how to frame her answer. "I might have been seen following Vincent when I got the license plate number."

She watched a glance go between the two detectives. Then Watson turned back to her. "You are stepping too close to some dangerous territory, Ms. Duchesne."

"That's basically what he said." Monique stood, tired of feeling like a kid being lectured by the principal. "So you came here for something."

"We need to ask you to come down to the station," Watson said.

Monique was in no mood for riddles. "Why?"

They glanced at each other again, and Monique decided she wasn't going anywhere with them unless she had her answer, or a lawyer. "Gentlemen, I have had a shitty couple of days. I want to go home and get some food and sleep. If you want me to come with you, you need to tell me why, or arrest me."

"You aren't under arrest, but we need you to come to the station, and tell us what you know about a murder that occurred yesterday."

Three murders in as many days, and the cops somehow think this new one was connected to her. How had she gotten this close to the vicious side of the world? Why had Alexi chosen to move across the hall for her apartment? "Why do I have to come to the station?"

"I don't think you want to discuss this here. And the crime scene team is in your building right now."

Monique's legs gave out as she took in what he said. "In my building? Is Mac okay? Is it someone I know?"

Watson took her elbow and led her back to the chair. "We'd like to find that out. Will you come to the station now?"

13

Monique let them take her to the station on Main and Keefer. They led her to same room she'd been in two days ago. This time Watson brought tea and a packaged chicken sandwich. "It's not great, but it's food."

She put the sandwich to the side, too keyed up to be hungry, and tested the tea. It was perfect, scalding, sweet, black, and it did help. "Can we get this over with?"

"Can you tell us where you were yesterday morning?" Adams asked.

How can they say she's not a suspect, but ask her that kind of question? "I was a lot of places yesterday morning. What time?" She hoped it wasn't around the time she was in Alexi's apartment. Had someone seen her go in despite the precautions she took?

"We think this happened around ten, maybe as early as nine." Watson seemed to have switched to good cop. If they were trying to put her off balance, it wasn't working. As far as she was concerned, they were both bad cop.

She decided to let them play their game. If the victim was

anyone she knew it wouldn't get any worse for waiting. "I was having breakfast at Mitch's diner. You can check with Jack."

"Did you see anyone going into the apartment when you left?" Watson locked his eyes on her face.

Monique considered lying, but there were already too many lies for her to keep straight. "Yes. Some guy was looking for Alexi. He asked me if I'd seen him. I told him Alexi was dead, and he should talk to you if he had any questions."

Detective Adams took a picture out of the file folder he was holding. "Is this him?"

Monique kept her eyes on Adams, afraid to look at the picture. If it was the man she'd spoken to, and Vincent had killed him, it was going to be bad. She didn't want to have a panic attack if there was blood. Not in front of the cops. The trembling was already starting with just the anticipation of what she might see. She clasped her hands together in her lap so the detectives wouldn't see, and probably misinterpret, her reaction. "How bad is it? I'm not good with gore."

"It's just his head. No blood." He pushed the photo closer. "We need to know if this is the man you saw."

Monique took a breath and looked down. Adams hadn't lied, although she wouldn't put it past him to do it just to see how she reacted. She saw the shaved head. She saw the scar still pulling on his face. "Yes, it's the man I saw." She pushed the photo back toward Adams. "Do you know who he is?"

"Yes, a local criminal named Marek Prochazka. It looks like he broke into the apartment. A few things were moved around in the bedroom. Someone must have come in while he was tossing the place. They stabbed him and left him to bleed out."

The memory of the blood in the center of the carpet flashed before her eyes. "Thanks for the details." She picked up her purse. "I'm going now." She wasn't going to stay here and break down. If she could get outside, the fresh air might help stem the darkness.

"We'll get a car to take you home," Watson said, walking around to open the door.

Monique strode through before saying, "No, I'm taking a cab." Being in a cop car would be just the same as staying here.

She pulled out her phone and called the taxi as she maneuvered through the crowd of people waiting in the corridor. She couldn't wait to get out of the station, the aura of desperation almost choking her.

When she got outside, the rain splashed across her face. It was freezing, but she waited on the street because she couldn't stay inside one more minute. Even standing in the tiny shaded area outside the door, made her feel too close to the violence and hate inside. The image of the man bleeding out wouldn't leave her, but, at least, outside she could breathe.

The cab arrived within five minutes. And ten minutes later she was closing her apartment door on the world.

Monique pressed her back against the door and rubbed her eyes with her still clenched fists. She'd run from the stairs to her apartment, keeping her eyes away from Alexi's door. In her imagination, blood was creeping across the hall.

This was getting worse. She couldn't even handle the thought of violence now. Was it just because of everything piling up? That after being safe for so long, it was all coming at her?

Monique dropped her hands from her face. She was not going to let this defeat her. She would get a grip on herself, and she would take her life back. She didn't need anyone to help her. She'd managed to put everything away inside before and start a normal life. She would do it again.

She knew that sleeping would help her to reset, that it would help her to get over the memory of two murders, and a threat, and Didi going through detox and... Monique stopped inventorying the reasons she wouldn't sleep.

Opening a bottle of wine, she grabbed a glass and curled up on the couch. She needed to decide how to move forward, how to get through whatever shit kept coming her way. She took a gulp of her wine, not caring what it tasted like, just needing the alcohol in her blood. If she decided to give the cops everything, would it be enough? What would they do with it? How would that keep everyone safe?

All she knew was that a war criminal was operating some kind of crime syndicate in Vancouver. Okay, maybe she didn't know, but she couldn't think of another explanation for everything. What seemed certain was his ability to hide. He was smart enough not to get his picture in the paper, or anywhere on the Internet since coming. Otherwise that app would have found him under another name or found other pictures she might have recognized.

Monique was certain it had to be about more than just stolen credit cards. It was hard to believe the killings were just about that. Surely a bullet would have done the job if they needed to keep someone from talking.

Then there was the weirdness of Vincent killing Snake just because he wouldn't deliver the bag of stolen cards.

Monique shrugged off the questions. This wasn't helping her sleep. All she had was things she knew, and she wasn't all that sure she knew them. There wasn't a trail to follow like in a mystery story. There was no pointer to show her the next step.

It all seemed so simple in books and movies. The heroine just snooped around and solved the problem. She didn't want to solve it. She didn't want to get involved. The problem was someone thought she was already involved.

Maybe she could just stop following Vincent. Whoever called might believe she had backed off.

She was backing off; she swore as she took another swallow of wine. If Didi were involved, she'd make sure he had a good lawyer. Andy had a point when he said she should stop enabling her brother.

Stretching out, Monique heard her joints crack. She reached for her cigarettes hoping they would relax her, before she remembered her decision to quit. She rolled herself in her throw and sipped the wine. If she could stop thinking about Vincent and the Colonel, maybe she'd be able to at least get in a nap before she had to do anything else.

Her thoughts kept breaking into her attempts to sleep.

She wasn't sure about Vincent. If he was working for The Colonel, then why did he want Snake to deliver the bag? If he wasn't working for The Colonel, why did she get that phone call? Was that Vincent? It sounded like him, but she was going more on the accent than anything else because his voice in the alley was more alive than the voice on the phone.

Monique lay back on the couch. This was getting her nowhere. Pouring another glass of wine, she turned on her stereo and let the sounds of jazz float her into a calmer state. The playlist was only instrumental, which meant she could listen and not be tempted to sing with the vocalist. She could rest her voice because she didn't have a set at the club tomorrow. And given the phone call, she planned to stay away from The Blue Scene when she wasn't working.

She tucked a cushion under her cheek and took another sip from her glass. She was almost halfway through the bottle. It would probably make sense to stick a cork in it so it would stay, well not good, but drinkable. She just needed to close her eyes for a second.

. . .

SOMETHING WOKE HER. Her heart hammered until she heard a burst of laughter from the street. It was probably a car door slamming that had broken into her dreams, not a murderer smashing through her door. She'd fallen asleep on the couch in front of the open window.

She checked the display on her phone, no missed calls. It was almost three. She'd managed a couple of hours sleep. Now that she was awake, she was tempted to call Andy, but if he wasn't a night person, she might lose an ally. And if Didi were sleeping, she didn't want to wake him.

She'd have to trust Andy to call. It felt like a good place to start changing her life, with trust. She dropped the phone into her purse.

She rolled to a sitting position and her stomach rumbled. Glad she'd grocery shopped, Monique went to check that she'd locked her door before going to the kitchen, and then decided to check the windows. Everything seemed secure, but she wouldn't leave the front window open again.

She made herself a sandwich and poured a glass of milk. The acid in her stomach made her think the wine hadn't been such a good idea. Her nap was too short for a hangover to develop, but she could feel the dehydration settling in, and a headache wouldn't be too far behind if experience taught her anything.

The people who'd woken her had long disappeared behind their own closed doors and the world was silent again. This was her favorite time of night, or rather, the very early hours of the morning. When no one was hurrying to work, and most people had come home from the clubs. It was usually silent enough that she could hear the quiet rumble of traffic on Main Street and if it was misty, the mournful call of a foghorn. Tonight it was clear, and the traffic was light. The night had a magical quality of renewal, everything fresh and clean.

The sandwich gone, she wandered the apartment checking windows and doors again. Leaning in to look through the peephole to check that the hall was empty. The thought of going out later in the day to lead a walking tour gave her a twinge. If she wasn't careful, she'd become afraid to leave her apartment.

She realized it wasn't fear keeping her agitated. It was annoyance at herself for considering giving up on the investigation.

Yes, it was dangerous. No, she didn't have much real information. But she hadn't taken the time to look. All she'd been doing was thinking about confessing to breaking into the apartment just to off-load the responsibility.

Now that there'd been another murder, she couldn't tell the detectives about the picture. There was no way she'd look innocent. She could almost hear Detective Watson now. If she broke in once, she could have done it twice – well, she had – and if she did that, what proof would she have that she didn't commit the murders? All of them.

It was time to stop just reacting. She needed to get something she could hand over to the cops without implicating herself. She needed a plan. She needed to take some action.

Doing some on-line searches wouldn't be dangerous. It would be better to do that and try to give the cops something to work with, other than suspect her. And maybe if she could identify this killer, she could move on. She could focus on Didi, and Rafe, and her career.

Monique reached into her purse for her phone to start the search. The small screen made her wonder if it was time to get a laptop, or maybe a tablet. If she needed to go deep into research, she couldn't rely on her ability to read microscopic text.

The phone started vibrating as soon as she touched it. She flipped it over and answered it without looking.

"Monique?" Andy's voice was strained.

"What happened?" Her heart stopped while she waited for his answer. *If Didi was dead...* she couldn't complete the thought.

"Didi is having a hard time waking up." Andy's words caught as he tried to tell her what happened.

She pressed her lips together and swallowed the fear in her throat. "Will he wake up? Should I come there?"

She heard Andy breathe in, and realized he was suppressing the same emotions that she was, fear, and sadness. "There's a good chance he'll be okay. Sometimes it's just difficult for people to deal with the physical trauma. Even though he is under anesthetic, his body still goes through the withdrawal."

Monique didn't tell Andy he'd already explained it. Maybe it was helping him to talk it through. "Where are you? I'll come down and wait with you."

"No, it's going to be fine. He'll wake up soon. I know he will. He didn't want you here, Monique. He wanted to see you when he was well. I'm just overreacting."

"It's not about him, Andy. You sound like you could use some support." She didn't know what she would do when she got there, but maybe just holding his hand and being there would be enough.

"You shouldn't come. You know what Didi is like. If he finds out we didn't do as he asked... Anyway, thanks, but I think we should wait."

She knew exactly what her brother was like. He'd go into a snit. "Okay, if you're sure. Just call me when he comes out of it. Don't worry about the time. I'm going to be up for a while."

Andy promised and then ended the call.

Monique stared at the phone and tried not to think about life without Didi. Life completely alone. Didi wasn't exactly living in her back pocket, sometimes she didn't see him for months, but he'd always been there. She checked the volume on the ringer to make sure she'd hear the call when it came. Putting the phone on the counter, she tried to clear her mind of the darkness Andy's call had pushed her into.

Didi could take care of himself. He always had, and, despite his lifestyle, he'd survived some pretty bad shit. He was tougher than he looked, so he'd get through this. That's what she should have told Andy. That Didi was a survivor.

She grabbed her phone and typed *rapid detox* into the search bar. She needed to know more about what could go wrong.

After following links for ten minutes, Monique was no further ahead. The information was vague. Maybe he was just reacting to the anesthetic. Maybe he was too weak to get better. And maybe Didi was in a coma. And he would wake up anytime...or never. There was nothing she could do about it, and she couldn't go see him. It would be stupid to believe she could forget about Didi, but she might as well get back to her investigation.

She started to search for information on Serbian communities in Vancouver. The Colonel wouldn't be stupid enough to identify himself within the community, if he was smart enough not to have his image on-line. Monique didn't have much hope that she'd find him easily. What she hoped for was some hint as to where to look for clues.

What little information she could find seemed to link a lot of communities from Eastern Europe together. Vancouver was made up of many nationalities. While they eventually spread out over the whole Lower Mainland, most immigrant communities stayed together for a few years. Recently the preferred place for immigrants from the old Soviet states was within a few blocks of Monique's apartment.

That information gave her a starting place. She could walk the neighborhood, discreetly. She turned off her phone and took it with her to bed. She needed to try to sleep through the incipient hangover, before getting started on her research.

14

Despite Monique's efforts at keeping the hangover at bay, it was a painful morning. She felt as though every hangover she'd missed over her life had crashed on her in one avalanche of dehydration and alcohol poisoning. Aspirin, water, and a few slices of toast helped make her feel like venturing out but didn't make her feel good.

The rain had been blown away in the night and it was one of those rare winter days in Vancouver, the air crisp and fresh. Snow frosting the mountains but not the streets. Monique had a walking tour booked in Chinatown, so she had to pull it together.

She didn't have much hope of running into Vincent in Chinatown. It would be helpful if she could use the walk to get some information on The Colonel, she just didn't know how. The old families weren't the only people living in Chinatown. There were some new buildings around the edges where a sketchy element had moved in. Maybe she'd check them out later.

She had about two hours to search around the one neighborhood that did hold some hope. It was only ten blocks away, so it wasn't worth driving and then trying to find parking. If she were lucky, the walk would clear the last of the fuzz from her head as well.

Wanting to be as unencumbered as possible, Monique took her phone, a handful of cash, and her keys with her. She looked at the cigarettes and lighter, and then swept them into a kitchen drawer. She wasn't quite ready to throw them out, but if she didn't have them with her, perhaps today could be the first day she didn't have a cigarette.

Monique knew that giving up the habit wouldn't help Didi recover, but it couldn't hurt either.

Outside, the chill bit at her cheeks. She breathed in a lungful of icy air and blew it out before jamming her hands into the pockets of her winter jacket and heading north. The houses in her neighborhood were old, some restored, some badly renovated, and too many of them just crumbling away. It took her fifteen minutes of walking before she arrived in a triangular neighborhood formed where Kingsway curved east between Fraser and 12th.

The houses were tidy but shabby. No one was restoring homes on these streets like they were in other areas. Some of the yards had swing sets, and some were planted with vegetables – vegetable stumps and rotting leaves at this time of year. She heard a woman yelling at someone, the language sounded right, well, it sounded like Russian, or Polish. Monique wasn't sure she would recognize the right language if she did hear it.

Now she was in the area, she realized that she had no plan, and it would look suspicious if she just walked along the streets. She pulled her phone out and pretended to check something on the screen. Her face flushed with embarrassment at the stupidity of her ruse. Monique decided it would be better to go get a coffee. If she had something to hold, it might be easier to fake a reason to be there. There had to be something on

Kingsway. No Starbucks, they didn't seem to want to be in this part of Vancouver, but there were a few independent cafes around.

Monique turned the corner and blinked at the noise and rush of traffic that felt foreign after the quiet of the side streets. The aroma of freshly roasted coffee beans drew her attention. She tracked it to a small coffee shop a block away. Monique hurried through the heavy door and joined the line waiting to order. The tables were filled with men talking loudly, laughing, and slapping shoulders. They looked alike enough to be related, wide faces, sharp cheekbones, brown hair, and blue eyes. She tried not to stare, but they weren't paying attention anyway. They were focused on their conversations.

A slight nudge from behind made her move forward, but she could still see the men. The Colonel wasn't among them, unless he'd had drastic cosmetic surgery, neither was Vincent. She couldn't stay much longer, but this was definitely a good place to investigate later when she had more time.

"What can I get you?" A beautiful young woman behind the counter interrupted Monique's thoughts.

"An Americano, please." Monique handed a five-dollar bill to the cashier and dropped the change in the tip mug. Her drink took only a minute, and then she had no reason to stay.

Sipping the coffee, she smiled, it was excellent and fulfilled the promise the smell of roasting beans had made.

Two hours later, no further along in her search for the colonel, Monique waited for her tour group to gather. It was a mixed bunch, four employees of a design firm on a team building exercise, and a couple of single tickets. Team building exercises usually involved a barrage of questions in pursuit of some kind of prize. She would need to make sure that the two single ticket holders got enough of her attention that they felt as though they got their money's worth.

The last straggler showed up as Monique was handing out the maps. "Okay everyone, we'll head down to the gates to Chinatown and explore the historic sites. It won't be a hard walk today. Are we ready?"

Everyone nodded. Monique pasted on her smile and led them out to the street. It was going to be interesting. The two single tickets were a young man who had startlingly blue eyes and four missing teeth, and another man, older, pale with black curly hair. He was giving off an intense vibe. He kept his eyes on her, even when she was talking to someone else.

Monique shrugged off the feeling of threat. He was probably just paying attention to her information and she was getting paranoid.

"Well, let's get started. If you have any questions just call out and I'll do my best to answer you." No one asked anything as they passed through the ornate Millennium Gate, the entrance to Chinatown. She did notice that some of the young people were muttering as she spoke, as though they were repeating her speech. Weird, but not the weirdest group she'd encountered.

They got to the Sam Kee building. "So, when the City appropriated most of his land to build the street, Sam just built this anyway. The building is six feet wide, and the city's bathing house was in the basement."

"Miss," the older man said. "I heard there was a lot of sweatshops in this area. Were there any people held prisoner under the city, in places like this?"

"There were some pretty bad times here, so yes, probably. I don't know of any official stories about prisoners, or slaves, though I wouldn't be surprised if there were things like that happening now. Times don't change as much as we hope they do." Monique ignored the chill that trickled down her spine and started walking to the next location. "If we could find out some information on that kind of history, I'm sure the company would start another tour. Would you be interested in something like Shameful Secrets of the City?"

He smiled. "Sure, why not."

Monique led them deeper into Chinatown, and they visited a few of the import stores where the young women bought red fans, and the men bought blue embroidered slippers. When they stopped for a snack at the Keefer Bakery, where usually coconut buns were the most popular snack on the tour, the younger members all ate the egg tarts, something Monique found too greasy. She decided the team building part of the day was to complete a series of odd tasks. Too bad she didn't know what they were. If the company had passed on that information, Melanie would have set up the tour to make it more challenging.

"Was there gang activity here?" It was the older guy again. This was the fifth time he'd asked about something like that. She'd have to let Melanie know that it might be a good idea to do a crime tour.

"Yes," Monique answered. "Like most port cities, we have our share of gangs. Chinatown was not immune." His questions were starting to bother her, but she shook it off. This guy didn't have an accent, so he was not likely to be related to the phone call.

They ended the tour outside the Walk in the Past office. Monique gave the sales talk about other tours available, and then the group dispersed. The team-building leader gave her a hundred dollar tip, the young guy grinned and handed her a five. The older guy glared at her and walked away.

Melanie, the owner of the tour company, offered Monique the opportunity to lead a second tour that had been booked that evening. "It's a group of women on a happy divorce evening. They want to end up at the Police Museum, there's a thing on there, an autopsy seminar or something. It'll be an easy one. You know this stuff by heart and there'll be some big tips. I'm pretty sure the women will already be tipsy by the time they arrive."

"Sure, I'll be back in half an hour, okay?" Monique needed a break to shake off the creepy feeling. The more she thought about it, the more she was sure the older guy wasn't on the tour to learn about the history of Chinatown.

There was a Waves Coffee House a few blocks away. She wanted to call Andy because it felt like Didi was punishing her by keeping silent. He must have come out of the detox by now. Even if he'd told Andy not to call, she could find out if he was okay.

And maybe she could call the police and find out if there was any headway on the murders, or the threatening call. Or maybe her conscience was pricking her to tell them about the damn picture.

She settled down at a table in the window to watch the activity on the street while she called. Until she found The Colonel, she was going to make sure she had the best view whenever she could. Vancouver was more like a small town than a city. Eventually you'd run into someone you were looking for if you were patient. She wanted to make sure that she wasn't surprised by someone seeing her first. After all, if the call had come from The Colonel, he knew what she looked like. He probably felt safe in his anonymity, so the picture gave her a slight advantage.

Monique picked at a blueberry scone as she watched the action on the street putting off the calls until she felt ready to hear the news, good or bad from either source. There was a mix of businesspeople, tourists, residents, and drug dealers to observe. The residents were young and hip, or old and poor, the tourists had the deer-in-the-headlights look of someone who had taken a wrong turn and weren't sure they were safe any longer. The drug dealers mostly just stood around on the corner in groups.

She dialed Andy's number first. If he had news, it would stop her worrying about Didi, and maybe it would help her lose some of the other stress at the same time. His voice mail came on. No news was the least desirable option.

"Hi, Andy, I know you said you would call, but I'm worried. I don't care if you have nothing to tell, please let me know what's going on. Thanks."

The scone was suddenly too dry to swallow, even with a mouthful of her coffee. Monique rubbed her eyes, feeling tears push and not wanting them to fall in public. Crying wasn't going to help Didi, and it had never helped her. She wrapped the scone in a napkin. There would be someone on the street who needed the calories more than she did.

When she had her emotions under control, she called Detective Adams.

"Adams."

It was a relief to get him. She didn't feel like playing games with Detective Watson. Adams at least played good cop well. "It's Monique Duchesne. I was hoping you had some information on that call I got."

"We haven't heard back from Telus about the call logs. Have you had any other incidents?"

Should she tell him about the creep? There was really nothing concrete. Just like everything in this case. Until she made some connection, it could all be in her imagination. Maybe the guy was researching a book, or just interested in weird things. The ice she could feel in her bones said it was a warning, and not just a coincidence. "Not really," she said finally, hedging her bets. "I'm just jumpy and I'm having trouble sleeping. It's not great thinking I'm going to be the next body you find bleeding out."

"I don't think it will come to that, Ms. Duchesne."

Irritation made her ask, "Why? If you have a good reason for me to stop worrying, I'm happy to hear it. I could use one less problem to deal with."

"No need to get upset. We don't think you have to worry because this guy's MO doesn't seem to be, make threats, and then wait. If he wanted you dead, you'd be dead, and we'd know about it. This guy isn't hiding his victims."

Did that make her feel better? Not really. How did they know that Vincent, or The Colonel, hadn't warned Alexi, or Snake, or even the last guy to end up dead in the apartment? "Will you let me know if you find out who called?"

"We'll call you in to identify his voice if we get enough information to arrest someone. But I wouldn't hold out too much hope. These guys use toss away phones. I would be very surprised if we could find him from the call."

"My tax dollar at work." Monique regretted her tone as soon as the words were out. "I'm sorry; I shouldn't take this out on you."

"Don't sweat it. You need to let us know if something changes. If you get another call, or someone suspicious is hanging around."

Monique opened her mouth to tell him about the creepy guy. The words wouldn't come out. When it came down to it, she didn't trust the cops. She knew that's why she'd been hanging onto the information. It wasn't because she couldn't think of a good lie about her visit to the apartment. She would rather put herself in danger than trust the cops to do their job. "No, nothing has changed." She ended the call.

Monique checked her phone for the time. It had been ten minutes since she sat down. She hated this feeling of hanging around waiting. She was waiting for news about Didi, waiting to hear from the cops about Snake's killer, and waiting for the next move from the person who threatened her.

She couldn't do anything about Didi, and she knew he was safe with Andy. She had to believe that. She could continue to look for The Colonel, but he was like a needle in a stack of needles right now. One thing she could do was find out about the creepy guy on the tour.

Melanie would have his registration form. It was only a matter of getting her hands on it. Melanie might not want to give her a client's private information, but if Monique offered to watch the office and give Melanie a break, she could easily find what she needed.

She put her empty mug on the counter and left. A teenager was huddled in a doorway in the next block. She handed him the scone and walked back to the office to prepare for her next tour and get the information she needed on the creep.

When Monique arrived back at the office, Melanie was on the phone so she couldn't just start sorting through the paperwork. It was only fifteen minutes until the divorce party was set to arrive and Monique knew that if she didn't get a chance to see the registration form now, she might never get to. This would be the last tour of the day. At the end of her shift, her job was to toss her time sheet through the mail slot and go home. Melanie would have put the receipts in the safe by the morning.

"'Kay, bye." Melanie hung up the phone after a few minutes. "Wow, I don't know what happened in the universe, but I've been taking calls all night for bookings. I guess this time the brochures we got into the hotels are really doing their job."

Monique pasted a big smile on her face. "That's great. Do you need any help? I can file or something until the tour arrives." It sounded so obvious to her ears, but maybe that was because she knew why she was offering.

"You don't need to do that, Monique," Melanie said. "I can take care of it tomorrow."

Monique wasn't going to give up that easily. "I have nothing else to do. How about I get you a coffee?"

"I'll never get to sleep if I take in any caffeine now." Melanie glanced at the front door. "Could you cover for a couple of minutes while I run to the little girl's room?"

"Sure. I can just take a message if someone calls, right?"

Melanie gestured toward a locked drawer. "Yeah, I'll be back before anyone needs to get into the cash. Thanks, Monique. If this keeps up, I'm going to have to hire someone to help with registrations. Back in a minute."

Monique nodded and leaned casually on the counter. Her every move felt like she was telegraphing her intentions.

As soon as Melanie was out of sight, Monique looked under the counter. It was like a cabinet, three drawers along the top, a cupboard under the left two drawers, and two shelves under the drawer on the right. Drawers and cupboard had locks. She gave each a small tug, all locked.

Glancing over her shoulder to make sure Melanie wasn't coming down the hall, Monique sorted through the contents of the shelves, brochures, and blank sign-up forms. What she needed was definitely behind one of the locks. On the top shelf, Monique found an Altoids tin. Prising it open, she found a single key on a ring. The key was small enough to fit the locks. She only had a minute or two and didn't want to take the man's signup form away, so she'd need to copy the information.

She opened the first drawer, a cash box. Monique closed and locked the drawer. The next one held Melanie's purse. The third one held what looked like the lost and found. Time was running out.

The cupboard lock stuck, and Monique's stomach tightened. She wiggled the key with one hand and unlocked her phone with the other. The door gave, and she saw a pile of completed forms. Hoping Melanie hadn't sorted them into some particular order, Monique quickly separated the ones with women's names and took a picture of each of the other forms.

As she locked the cupboard, the phone rang. Dropping the key into the tin and pushing it to the back of the shelf, Monique picked up the phone.

"A Walk in the Past, how can I help you?" She slid her phone into her pocket, nodded at the group of women entering the small office, and reached for a pen to take a message. She felt Melanie's presence just before the man on the phone asked her about booking a private tour. "Just a second, I'll pass you on to Melanie."

She ignored the conversation on the phone to greet the women she'd be taking around downtown for the next hour and a half. As her heart slowed to a normal place, Monique said, "Ladies. Are we ready to go?"

15

Two hours later, Monique sat on her couch looking at the four pictures on her phone, ready to delete the ones that were not creepy guy. He hadn't shared his name with the group, but the other three had, it was just a matter of remembering which names matched with the younger guys.

She closed her eyes and thought back to the introductions. The four young kids had gone first; introducing themselves like they were couples. Emily and Todd, yes he'd been the redhead. Alex had been the skinny one with the acne scars. The other two names, Drago Cakic and Rad Divac, had the right sound to be involved with The Colonel, but neither of them had accents. At least she only had to follow up on two names. Monique checked the addresses. They were almost at opposite ends of the city.

She closed her eyes. All the young guy had said was his name. She couldn't tell if he had an accent. Rad was short enough for that, and it could be a street name. If he'd said, Drago, would she have heard an accent? Maybe. Well, all she could do was check out both addresses. She'd start with Rad's address because her gut said the creep was Drago, and she wasn't ready to follow her gut just yet.

It was still early enough to go and check out the places without seeming weird driving past houses. Rad's address was across town. It was probably a basement suite given the 1/2 in the address, fifteen minutes' drive at most at this time of day. Monique grabbed a coat and her keys and headed out before she could change her mind.

The address was in the middle of a street lined with Vancouver specials. Houses built between the sixties and eighties. They were designed to have a rental suite on the ground floor, legal or not. Rad's home was lit up with the curtains drawn back and all Monique needed was for him to walk by the window. She sat in her car for what seemed to like too long to go unnoticed. She was craving a cigarette but was glad she'd left them at home.

Then the light dimmed inside, leaving only a flickering that meant the TV was on. Was he settled for the night? Monique didn't relish the thought of sitting outside the house until morning. If he didn't have a day job, he might not come out. She slid down in her seat, reluctantly preparing to spend the night. She wished she'd thought to get a coffee on the way, and then she regretted the thought as her bladder twinged. "I'm not cut out for this stakeout thing."

The TV was backed up against the window, blocking half the space. The flashes of light gave Monique the impression that he was watching an action movie. The flickering light made Monique blink, and each blink was a little slower. It was chilly and she was starting to doze off. She pinched her thigh to keep alert.

She was tempted to drive away, but she couldn't just leave now. If this was her guy, she needed to know. Even if he wasn't, well then she'd know it was Drago and that meant she could figure out her next move. She decided to stay for an hour. If Rad didn't move within that time, she'd go looking for the other address.

She looked at the pictures of the receipts again. No phone numbers so she couldn't make him move by calling. She couldn't knock on the door; he would recognize her. Even if he wasn't the creep, she'd have a hard time explaining what she was doing there.

She kept checking her phone for the time. Over the next half hour, the flashing from the TV stopped three times. Each time Monique held her breath but the shadow of someone moving never resolved into a face in the window.

Monique realized she wasn't going to be able to sit for the full hour. The intervals between checking her phone were getting shorter. Rad didn't seem to need to come to the window, and she was going to have to move on and hope that it wasn't a mistake.

She gave herself five more minutes and sat on her hands to stop them reaching for the phone every thirty seconds. The TV went dark a moment later. Then Rad appeared in the window. Monique started the car and pulled away. Rad was the young guy.

The address Drago had given was out near Hastings Park, almost in Burnaby. The rain had started up again, making it difficult to see the lines on the road. Monique rarely drove, and even less often at night, because she had problems seeing clearly in the glare of traffic. The oncoming headlights seemed to be running on high beam the whole way. Tension had her gripping the steering wheel so tightly her hands ached. She tried to ease her hold, but it wasn't until the next red light that she could release the wheel and shake out the stiffness in her fingers.

Arriving at the address, Monique was glad of the rain. It meant that no one was wandering the street, and the few residences were tightly locked behind drawn curtains and blinds. There would be no witnesses to her lurking.

Parking under a burned out streetlight, she stared at the building. It seemed to be an old warehouse turned into a collection of offices. She couldn't count on seeing Drago unless he visited closed businesses at night in the rain. And she was suddenly unsure that he'd be likely to have given a real address, or name.

Monique decided to wait anyway. There was nothing to do at home but worry about Didi, and she could do that in the car just as easily as at home. She'd stopped on the way at a gas station to use the bathroom, so she wouldn't have any distractions.

Monique scanned the windows of the building. Each had signs about the businesses that occupied the office. It was an eclectic group, none of which were War Criminals Incorporated. There was a web design company, a building developer, and a caterer. The other three companies had names so weird that she had no idea what they produced.

There were lights on at the caterer, A Taste of Home, and at the web design company, Yoursite.com. Everyone else had gone home. Maybe the creepy guy was just a socially awkward computer geek. She couldn't find a way to make herself believe that. And it was too dangerous to ignore the questions he'd asked. If she was going to investigate, Monique decided she would believe her gut and think of him as a threat.

After a few minutes, she saw movement on the street. It was a couple of men walking toward the building, one too short to be Drago, and the other too fat. Both wore hoodies against the drizzle, and they seemed to be talking quietly. The lights went out at the web design company as the men approached. They glanced around before entering the building. The fat guy tossed a butt into the gutter. A few seconds later, two young women exited the building, popped up umbrellas, and walked toward the lights of Hastings.

So something was going on at the caterer. Were they prepping for tomorrow? Or was this something more sinister? Monique had hoped that following up on Drago would answer some of her questions, not create more.

Over the next half hour, six more men made their way into the building. A caterer that only employed men didn't feel legitimate. Monique didn't know what to do next. Staying in the car seemed like a waste of time. Going home felt unsatisfying. What she really wanted to do was snoop. Go look in a window and see what was going on. If it was just a catering company, then she could go home. If it was something else... maybe she'd give the information to the cops and go home.

Was she ready to take the chance and go look? As much as she hated to admit it, Rafe was right. Monique had lived too long trying to safeguard herself, to keep others out. She'd never had her privacy threatened before.

She knew that whatever was pushing her to find out who was behind the killings was part self-preservation. Not knowing what the police were doing to catch the murderer was feeding her need to take control. She had no doubt that the threat was real, but she was seeing danger in every little quirk, and that was not a safe way to live either.

Monique scanned the street. There was no movement. No one had come toward the building for at least ten minutes. The rain had stopped. She had to find out if she was just paranoid about Drago, or if her sense of survival was telling her the right thing.

She stepped out of the car and hunched into her jacket. Leaving the car unlocked, and holding her ignition key ready to use, Monique walked to the end of the street.

She hoped there was a handy back alley she could use to spy from. If not, she would have to try looking through the front window. That felt both dangerous and idiotic.

When she turned the corner, her heart lifted. A service alley led back halfway down the block before turning right to empty onto the parallel street. The only light came from the window of A Taste of Home, and it was right at the turn of the alley.

She would be visible to anyone looking out, but no one seemed to be paying attention to the alley. The left side was almost completely dark. She might be able to get away with it. If she moved her car to the parallel street and came from that direction, it would mean she wasn't approaching the building head on, which should make her safer.

Monique did a quick check that she wasn't being watched, and then walked back to the car, forcing herself not to run and bring attention to her actions.

The next block was mixed residential and commercial properties, which meant that, at this time of night, everyone was home and their cars were parked on the street. She took the chance and pulled in next to a hydrant, then made her way to the alley. Monique relaxed a fraction of the tension that held her tight. This side of the alley was much better for sneaking up on the building. Two dumpsters cast shadows and provided quick nooks for hiding in an emergency.

Monique sidled along the alley. Her heart banging in her chest, she felt the pulse in her throat and lips and fingers. She didn't even try to calm it, she just kept moving.

She saw a deep shadow between the electrical pole and a garage at the corner of the alley. If she slipped in beside the electrical pole, she'd be able to see most of the interior of the lit room. The danger was being seen as she crossed the space between the last dumpster and the pole.

Her mouth went dry at the thought of being caught. Now she

was here, the reality of what she was doing sank in. She stood as still as she could and tried to think. Panic shivered in at the edge of her perception.

The longer she was in the alley the more danger that someone would do something about her car. Like call the police. She realized that if she went back to the last dumpster, she could cross more safely, but it was adding delay to her limited time. Monique stopped dithering and made her way back through the shadows to cross the alley, and then stepped carefully through the weeds and mud at the edge of the paving until she was safe in the darkness beside the pole.

Watching the activity in the room across the way, Monique could see about three quarters of the room and from about hip height up. It was definitely not a catering business. There was a big table. Men were seated around it, some drinking from mugs, and others from shot glasses. They were looking at someone sitting out of her line of sight.

Monique couldn't help feeling like she was on display. Some of the men seemed to be staring right at her. She calmed the rising panic by telling herself that they would be reacting if they could see her. None of them so much as changed position, so she felt safe enough to watch.

At the far side of the table, Drago sat with a bottle at his elbow. He was definitely not a socially awkward geek. In this setting his menace was painted all over his face. That, and his body language, erased any lingering doubt that he was innocent. Despite everything, Monique still had nothing she could give to the cops.

It wasn't illegal to pretend to be a caterer. It also wasn't illegal to ask creepy questions.

Her feet were freezing and wet. The cold creeping up her legs and sapping her will to stay. She kept her eyes on the window as she started to shift her weight to begin her escape to her car. No one seemed to notice the movement. They continued to listen to whoever was talking. Monique was almost around the power pole when Vincent walked into the room.

She froze.

He couldn't see her. She didn't know if she was telling herself or praying to anyone who might be listening.

He took the bottle from beside Drago and reached for one of the glasses in the middle of the table. Pouring himself a shot, he raised his glass toward the unseen person in the corner and tossed the contents back. Wiping his mouth with the back of his arm, he took a chair and leaned back.

Taking a shaky breath in, Monique inched away from the corner. As soon as she was sure she was out of sight, she ran to her car.

MONIQUE WAS SHAKING SO BADLY she had to pull over into the parking lot of a McDonald's. It took her a few minutes to stop trembling and clear her mind enough to pay attention to the road again. Far from feeling satisfied that she'd found something out, Monique was terrified. She couldn't feel the compulsion to investigate through what was becoming a familiar panic attack.

What the hell was she doing?

Was she crazy?

Three murders and two threats – there was no doubt in her mind that Drago had been threatening her – and she acted like she was some kind of super sleuth.

Monique badly wanted a cigarette, but she wasn't going to buy them. She couldn't have a drink until she got home. She'd never been a nervous eater, so McDonald's didn't have anything that would calm her nerves. What she needed to do was talk to Rafe. At this point, she was willing to apologize for anything as long as she didn't have to be alone.

After about five minutes, the trembling had subsided enough for her to drive, so she started the car and pulled out into traffic. At this time of night, it was mostly taxis taking people home from clubs. They were driving sanely, so she could concentrate on her own driving rather than worry about everyone else.

As she drove, Monique gave herself a pep talk. "Don't argue with him. Apologize and leave your ego out of it. It's okay to like someone, not everyone will betray you." She'd given this speech to herself many times over the years. Each time she did, she tried to believe it. Every time up to now, her instinct had been proven right as people betrayed her over and over again.

Parking outside Rafe's apartment building, Monique looked up to his window. There was a faint light leaking through the blinds. He was awake, at least. She swallowed a feeling of regret that she needed to see him because she was afraid that she had to admit she couldn't deal with everything on her own, that she had gotten in over her head.

He buzzed her in without comment. When the elevator door opened, he was waiting for her. "You look like shit. Come on, it's warm in my place."

Monique reached for his arm, but he had already turned away. She followed him to his door and walked through as he held it open. His gas fireplace was turned on and, by the warmth that flowed over her, it had been on for hours. The chill in her bones was replaced with a weariness that had her crawling onto his couch.

"Wine?"

"Please."

He handed her a glass then looked closely at her face. "Have you eaten?"

"Today?" When he didn't laugh, she added, "I could eat, I guess."

Rafe didn't answer, just went to the kitchen, and started banging around.

Monique fought to keep her eyes open. The shock and the cold were enough to explain the way she felt. Between sleepless nights, threats, and worry about her brother, it was no wonder she was out of energy. The next thing she knew, Rafe was poking her awake.

"It's just an omelet. Eat then tell me what happened to make you look like death warmed over."

He sat across from her and stayed silent until she put the last bite in her mouth.

"Okay, Monique, talk. And don't pretend it is all okay. I know you."

She considered everything that had gone bad in her life recently. "It's hard to know where to start. I guess a good place is that you and I are fighting again. I'm sorry about that. Can we call a truce?"

"Maybe. Keep talking." Rafe wasn't being hard on her to be an asshole. Monique saw the twitch of the muscle in his jaw. He was holding back his anger to give her a chance. It was a good sign that he was trying to let her talk before reacting. And maybe his anger was a good sign too. It meant he cared.

She started with the easiest stuff. Stuff he couldn't expect her to control. "Didi is not coming out of the anesthetic. At least that's the last I heard from Andy."

He reached for her knee and patted it. "I'm sorry to hear that. I hope he'll be okay. You don't need more family trauma. I don't think that's all, though. Keep talking."

Monique knew she should just tell him, but the words were too hard to get out. "I can't remember how much I told you about the murder, or rather murders."

"You should probably start at the beginning. Pretend I don't know anything."

Monique told Rafe everything that had happened over the last few days. As she heard the story unfold, she realized how bad it sounded. Living it had been harrowing, but hearing it was almost worse. Halfway through Rafe moved to the couch and wrapped her in his arms. The rest of her words were spoken into his chest. "So I don't know what to do. The cops aren't interested. I can't just sit back and wait for these guys to decide I need killing."

He pulled back to look in her eyes. "Just because they aren't keeping you up-to-date doesn't mean that the police aren't investigating. Call them and tell them what you saw. Let them deal with it. They have guns and training."

"And if they don't take it seriously?"

"You won't know until you call. Do that and we'll figure out the next steps."

She felt the reluctance crawling back into her gut. "I doubt either of them will be working at this time of night. I'll do it tomorrow."

Rafe's muscles tightened.

Monique drew away. "I should go. You're probably busy."

He let her wriggle out of his arms. "You can stay here tonight."

"I need to go home. I can't let them push me out of my home, Rafe. No matter what the cops do, or don't do. I need to know I can still be alone."

"I don't like the idea of you being so close to where two people were murdered. Your neighbors are no help. Mac is only interested in getting as many one-night stands into a week as possible, and the others might as well not even live there. Stay here. Just for tonight."

She pulled away and stood. "No, I need to go."

"Call me when you've talked to the cops."

Monique knew he meant it to sound caring, but it felt like he didn't trust her. "I will." She wasn't sure that she was telling the truth. "I have to go, Rafe."

He nodded and picked up her dishes. "Don't do anything stupid, Monique."

She shrugged into her jacket and picked up her purse. "I'll try not to."

16

When Monique woke the next day, she felt rested. For her, seven hours sleep was a luxury and showed how much she'd been drained by the events leading up to last night. She called Detective Adams, more to hold up to her promise to Rafe than because she thought it would make a difference. He'd told her to stay out of it and wouldn't give her any details about their investigation.

The lack of details made her more convinced that they weren't doing a thorough investigation. That a bunch of criminals getting murdered was the lowest priority. Even so, she still couldn't bring herself to tell them about the picture she'd taken from the apartment. It wasn't going to help anyone sitting in a file on Watson's desk.

Detective Adams had told her they would look into the catering company. She hadn't found comfort in that promise, and he hadn't made any effort to give her any. He'd gotten off the phone as soon as he could.

Then she left another message for Andy. If he didn't call back soon, she'd start tracking down detox centers and find Didi on her own. If Didi didn't want to talk to her, the least he could do was let her know what happened – and pick up his stuff.

By the time she turned up for her shift at the club, Monique was ready to bite the head off the next person who didn't do what she expected. The walk to the club hadn't cooled her off much, and anger didn't do anything good for her voice. Pulling the cigarettes out of her purse, Monique lit up and walked around the block as she smoked. She tried to shake off the annoyance with the world, but the fact that she was smoking again added to her frustration. Nothing was working to lift the mood that she'd woken in.

She flicked the stub of her cigarette into the gutter and worked her way through the crowd into the musician's lounge. In her head, she was counting to ten, not wanting to take out her anger on the guys. She wasn't sure why her frustration had turned to anger, but there it was. She walked in and stopped dead in her tracks. Ray was dancing with Wes. Ali quietly playing a waltz on the double bass.

The sight of the two old men fighting to lead, all elbows and grins, bubbled laughter from deep inside, melting her anger on the way out. She was finally able to squeeze out words between gasps of laughter, "Am I missing something?"

The music stopped. Ray and Wes bowed to each other before collapsing on the chairs.

Ray flicked his fingers at Ali. "Our friend here has some news."

Monique raised an eyebrow and waited.

Ali carefully laid his instrument against the desk beside him. Keeping his eyes on his hands, he said, "I got a call from the symphony. They need me to fill in for a couple of weeks."

"So he had to practice his classical repertoire, and we were helping him with timing," Wes said.

"But I think he was playing a waltz, and it looked like you were dancing a polka."

Wes grinned. "I'm more of a free spirit. The constraints of the dance world will not shackle my moves."

Ali winked at her. "It's a good thing I wasn't watching them for help, although it's hard to concentrate on playing an instrument when you're laughing your ass off. How are you doing, Monique?"

"Better now. I'm happy for you, Ali. When do you start?" She hoped they would have time to rehearse with a new band member.

"Next week. Don't worry I've lined up a friend to fill in. You'll like her. She's coming by in a couple of days."

Monique stretched out the last bit of tension in her body. "Cool, I'm sure she'll be almost as good as you. Why don't we do an evening of your favorites to celebrate? What would you like for the first set?"

"I've never been in charge of the song order before," Ali said. "How about we start with *Stormy Weather*?"

They spent the last hour before their set running through every song Ali proposed. Monique was relieved that he loved the standards. She knew them all well enough to sing on demand. It was a good way to send Ali off to the symphony, but Monique couldn't help feeling as though he was leaving her the way everyone had left her, all her life.

THE AUDIENCE HAD WARMED to the performance. The first set had gone well, and their second set had done even better. Monique followed Ray off the stage to get her purse. It was hard to think about going home to her empty apartment after such a great show. An empty apartment didn't always feel like home even without murder and threats.

She said goodnight to the guys who were staying to back up Maisie. The girl had hit big with the regulars. Monique took her jacket and the rest of her belongings with her to the bar, this time she wouldn't be caught without her phone if something happened.

As she slipped past the tables scattered through the club, she noticed one particular table near the door. Five of the men she'd seen in the building last night were sitting there with Vincent. She tried not to react, but cold sapped her control as the fight or flight response pulled blood from her extremities.

She touched the back of the chair for balance as her world spun. She felt like she was alone, that Vincent was looking directly at her. The room went silent, at least for her. She felt the vibration of noise through her fingers on the chair, but no sound. She clutched the chair harder and tried to focus on the reality of the situation, not let her fears twist what she saw.

Vincent wasn't looking in her direction. He was watching the stage, smiling.

Monique forced herself to follow his gaze. Maisie was taking her place in the center. The girl had learned something about show business in the day since Monique had seen her. Afro pinned into a pleat, Maisie was wearing a tight black dress that only came halfway down her thighs, leading to black stockings, and stilettos. She had the looks and talent that meant a future, if she could stay clean.

The sounds started to come back as Monique allowed herself to believe that Vincent wasn't here to kill her. That the timing was a coincidence.

She'd have to warn Maisie about handling the wrong kind of fan later. But, maybe, she could get the cops to take Vincent off the street for a while. She dug into her purse as she changed direction to go out to Main Street. Suddenly home seemed like a safer option than the public bar.

She pressed the redial on Detective Adams' number as she wove her way out through the crowd, the opening notes of *What a Wonderful World* hushing the chatter.

"Detective Adams?" Monique had not been able to hear the words snapped as someone answered the phone.

"No, this is Watson. Who's calling?"

Monique looked around. There was no convenient crowd to hide in because the smokers had gone inside to enjoy the show. The road and sidewalk were wet, but the rain had stopped, and the clouds had blown away so she could see clearly. She stepped into the shadow of a doorway as she identified herself. "The man who killed Snake is in The Blue Scene right now. He's wearing a black leather jacket and black pants, and a white shirt. He's at a table near the door and there are five other men with him."

"We're on our way. Stay out of his sight." Watson ended the call.

Monique leaned back into the doorway. She wasn't going to move until she saw Vincent being taken out of the club in hand-cuffs. Then she'd feel safe. Of course, Tess wouldn't be happy about the disruption, or maybe it would boost her credibility to have an arrest on the property. Monique heard the faint sirens approaching as she leaned forward to watch the front door of the club. She darted back to the shadow as Vincent exited the club, phone to his ear.

He was only steps away. All it would take was a glance over his shoulder to pin her in his gaze.

She couldn't call Detective Watson because Vincent would hear anything she had to say. Monique held her breath and stayed motionless, willing Vincent to go back inside the club. She touched her phone, feeling for the volume button. Pressing it until she felt the vibration, Monique slid it into her purse. At least now, she didn't have to worry about Vincent being alerted if the police called her.

He didn't turn to look at anyone as he started walking downhill. He was still talking to whoever had called him from the club, and he didn't seem happy.

Monique waited until he was a block away before she slipped from the shadow of the door. She counted the steps until her next hiding place.

There was no way she was going to follow him openly. She'd learned her lesson from last time. There was no way she could stay and wait either. He would just slip away.

What if he had seen her in the club? During her set the house lights would have hidden him while she was on stage. What if he'd been there the whole time?

Fear chilled her more than the night could. She pressed her stomach as she moved, hoping to avoid being sick on the street.

The sirens were getting closer, but not fast enough.

Monique wondered if she could wave them down as they approached but shut down the idea of stepping out of cover so boldly – it was suicidal. She made it to the next doorway without Vincent noticing, or without him showing he'd noticed.

She pressed herself as deep into the shadow as she could and counted to five before peeking out. Vincent was nowhere in sight. She leaned out farther, and then glanced uphill in case his friends were coming to join him, but she was alone on the street.

The cops were close enough that she could see the flashing lights. She glanced one more time to where Vincent had disappeared, and then ran back to meet the cops at the club door.

There were four cruisers pulling to a stop when she arrived. Detective Watson stepped out of the only unmarked car and started to push his way through the crowd.

"Wait," she called to him. "He's not in there. He's down there somewhere." She pointed downhill. "I lost him a block away."

Detective Watson shook his head. "I told you to stay where you were."

Monique opened her mouth to explain, but he held up a hand to quiet her. "Save it." Then he directed the uniformed cops to search for Vincent. They pulled away silently with no flashing lights.

Watson turned back to her; fury blazed across his cheeks. "Are you determined to get yourself killed? Or don't you want us to find out who did this? "

"Yes, I mean no, but he was getting away. I was careful, and I was already outside." Monique wanted to slap him. Why was he trying to control her when he should be chasing down Vincent? "I need a drink. You know how to find me if you need me to identify him or something, right?"

He gave her a look she was sure he meant to be stern. It just looked annoyed to her. "This guy is probably gone already. I'll let you know if we find him. What do we need to do to stop you getting in our way?"

"I'm not getting in your way." Monique tried to keep her temper, but it was an uphill battle. "If it wasn't for me, you wouldn't even know about Vincent."

"Just be careful. I don't want to have to fill out the paperwork on your murder, okay?" He turned to go back to his car.

Monique was touched until she realized he really meant it about the inconvenience of the paperwork. "Sure. Just catch this guy and find out who's giving him his orders."

Watson turned to look at her. "What makes you think that someone is telling him what to do? Why can't he be working on his own?"

Monique forced a smile and tried to look innocent. She didn't need him to drag her to the station about the breaking and entering, and she had no doubt he would if she told him about it. "I find it hard to believe he's just killing people with no purpose. I guess he also doesn't strike me as someone who is in charge. I told you he mentioned some guy called The Colonel just before he killed Snake." To her own ears she sounded like she was hiding something. Wouldn't a detective hear the lies easily?

"Good point," Watson said. He gave her a hard look. "If there's nothing more, we have to try to catch this Vincent before he murders anyone else."

Monique kept her mouth shut and nodded before heading back to the warmth and noise of the club.

Tess was coming out as Monique slid past a group of customers who had rushed out to look at what caused the commotion. Tess glanced around at the now empty street, and then grabbed Monique's arm. "What's going on?"

"Nothing," Monique said without thinking. Then she looked at the worry on Tess's face. "It's nothing now, but we should probably talk."

Looking at Monique closely, Tess jerked her head toward her office door. "I think you're right. And we should talk now."

They worked their way through the crowd to the door tucked beside the bar. Tess had a small office, almost a closet, where she kept the books and did her payroll. Most of the time she worked in the office when the club was closed, so few people knew the room was more than a closet.

Monique followed Tess into the room and closed the door. When she turned back, Tess was sitting behind the metal desk ready to hear the story. Monique sat on the only other chair, one from the club that had a broken spindle in the back.

Tess didn't wait for Monique to figure out how to explain what was going on. "You've been acting weird lately. I know you saw Snake get killed, but it's more than that. You've been jumpy and this is the second time you've run out of the club after someone."

Monique rubbed her face to clear the exhaustion that had suddenly descended. "For the record, this time he followed me out." She shrugged at the words. They sounded petulant. "I'm not really sure what is going on. I've seen the guy who killed Snake here twice now. I've called the cops, but they can't seem to get here fast enough to catch him."

"So you called the cops to my club again?" Tess didn't sound happy.

"The guy is a killer, Tess. I can't just let him walk."

Tess flicked her fingers in dismissal. "I get that. What I don't get is why you are involved. Is there something I should know?"

Monique realized she needed to talk to someone about the whole series of events. Someone who wouldn't tell her to keep safe. Someone who might have a useful idea. Tess was pretty connected and despite what she'd said, she probably knew something. Maybe not about The Colonel, but about Vincent. She told Tess everything. "I guess now that these guys are coming into the club, it is making me even more jumpy. I don't like to think I've brought this here."

Tess pulled open a drawer in her desk and removed a bottle of whiskey and two shot glasses. She poured and then pushed one of the glasses toward Monique. She didn't say anything until both drinks were gone. The only thing filling the silence was the faint sound of voices from the club.

Monique was afraid that this was a goodbye drink. That Tess was getting ready to tell her that she was out of a job. Monique was in no hurry to hear that message.

Tess refilled her glass before speaking. "I don't know that you brought it here, but it's definitely here if Snake's killer keeps coming back. I figure it's only a matter of time before I get offered protection for a price." She tossed back the second shot. "The only way to avoid that is to deal with it. What table was he at?"

"I think it's table seven, the one just inside the door."

"Hang on." Tess wiggled her way around the desk and cracked open the door. "Four guys who look like the villains in a Steven Segal movie?"

Monique laughed. "Yes, exactly, what are you going to do?"

"Call in a few favors. We'll be the new after work drinking home for the cops. A few nights of unwelcome company should move them along." Tess settled back into her chair and offered Monique another shot.

"No, thanks, I think I'll be better off staying sober. So what do you think I should do?" It had felt good to tell Tess the whole story but feeling good wasn't going to get the murders solved.

"Give the cops the picture and tell them what you found out. Move in with Rafe until they get this guy."

Monique shook her head and stood. "Thanks anyway. I'll keep trying to find The Colonel."

Tess grinned. "I figured you would say that. Look, I don't know where this guy hangs out, but wherever it is, he'll be lying low. He'll be running things from behind someone. He can't afford to be noticed. War crimes don't have a statute of limitations, so to speak. My guess is that he's not afraid of incarceration as a war criminal. His type tend to rule in any violent environment. He's afraid of revenge. Of someone he tortured recognizing him. Or a relative of someone he killed."

Monique hadn't considered The Colonel would be hiding because he was afraid. "So even if the police get Vincent, The Colonel might still get away?"

"That's right. It sounds like you really want to get this Colonel guy. You need to know why you care about getting him. It's not because of Snake. You hardly knew him. It's something else, and that's what will get you through when it gets really dangerous."

"I think maybe Didi is in this somehow. And I can't ask him right now."

"If he is, you can't help him. I know you think you can, but his best bet is to go to the cops." Tess rubbed her forehead. "I hate this shit. I try to keep the club out of it, but gangs don't wait for an invitation."

Monique gave up trying to get information. Tess might know something, but there was no way she'd help Monique get deeper into danger. "I guess I'll just keep doing the same thing, and hope I get another idea before it's too late."

"Go talk to Rafe. You need to have a safe place to go. If Didi isn't really just sulking, you need Rafe to be there for you."

Monique knew Tess was right. The thing that kept her from talking to Rafe was the fear it would be another fight. She wasn't ready for that just yet. "I think I'll go hang out in the back for a while." Now that she'd told Tess, maybe she could ask questions of other people she trusted. Maybe Wes or Ray would know something from other clubs they worked. Some of those clubs were run by less than honest people.

"Just be careful. These guys could make a cornered rat look like Mother Teresa." Tess threw back another shot of whiskey and waved at the door. "Go ahead. I'll be out in a while."

Monique opened the door and glanced out. The men were gone. She slipped through and closed the door behind her.

The set was ending as Monique made her way past the stage into the back room. She tossed her purse on the desk and sank into the chair. Not smoking was screwing with her routines.

"Hey, I thought you left," Ray said as he walked into the room. "Can't get enough of us?"

"True, if you weren't in love with Wes, I'd be all over you." Monique smacked Ray's butt as he passed. "Where's Maisie?" She looked at the door. "In fact, where's everyone else?"

Ray dropped into the chair opposite her. "Having a drink. I

didn't feel like one. What's going on with you? I saw you leave like the devil was on your heels."

"I think he might be. I saw the guy who killed Snake, the guy in the alley, and I went out to call the cops." She paused. "I think he's connected with something bigger."

Ray looked up at her. "Ask what you want to ask. I'm making no promises, but I can't answer a question you haven't asked me."

Monique had been fretting over how get him talking. Since he'd been forthright, she decided to just ask. "Do you know anything about Serbian criminals in Vancouver?"

Ray sat back and looked at her, eyebrow raised. "There are some here, like any kind of community there are criminals and just regular people. What's going on, Monique?"

She gave him an abbreviated version of the facts. "It feels like I have to find this guy. It feels like something bad is coming. Or, I guess, something worse." Was that it? That she was seeing signs of coming violence that she'd missed with her father? Something that she should have seen, that could have stopped him.

"I'm sure that you're right. But, are you sure this isn't about Didi? You can't make him stay sober by taking out all the bad guys, Monique. There's always someone waiting to make a buck on misery."

Monique rubbed her face to clear the weariness. "No, it's not about that. I know Didi is responsible for his own choices."

"Okay, well some of the guys running the Queen Club are connected. I don't know if it's Serbian, but I can find out."

She went cold at the thought of putting her friends in danger. "Don't put yourself at risk. I hoped you knew something, but if you don't then leave it."

He reached over and patted her knee. "I know how to be careful, but I wasn't planning to ask any questions. You can learn a lot if you observe with an objective."

"Wes will kill me if anything happens to you."

"Nothing will happen. Now, I gotta go and make sure Wes gets something to eat. You want to join us?"

"No, I think I need to go make peace with Rafe." Tess was right about needing a place to go. She didn't want to go back to her apartment carrying this feeling that everyone was mad at her. Didi was either still unconscious or keeping her away because he was angry. Rafe, at least, would let her in. If she could keep her temper then they could talk. She'd stop using him as a safety net as soon as this was over.

17

The walk to Rafe's usually only took ten minutes. This time Monique felt like she was being followed, as if someone was about to stab her, or throw a garrote around her throat. Every minute of the walk felt like it took hours. She kept turning around hoping to catch someone, but no one was there. The feeling had her twitching by the time she buzzed Rafe's apartment.

"Come up." Rafe released the door as he spoke.

Monique slipped inside and watched the street from the back of the lobby. After a few minutes, she pressed the elevator call button. If she was being followed, they were experts and there was nothing she could do about it. As she rode the elevator, Monique wondered if she should tell Rafe about the feeling. She decided to keep quiet since there was no evidence. He'd only use it to tell her to stop looking for Vincent because it was making her crazy.

He was waiting for her at his door. She reminded herself to keep her temper and be reasonable, even if she had to hold back a few details.

She kissed his cheek as she passed. "I'm sorry we fought. I

don't want you to be mad at me." The words were becoming too familiar.

He wrapped his arms around her and kissed her. "I don't like it when we fight either. I'm sorry too." He squeezed her in a hug and walked with her to the living room. "Why don't we curl up on the couch and watch an old movie. If we don't talk, we can't fight."

"Popcorn?" Maybe he was right. They could just pretend that everything was normal, and it would be. There was no need to drag up anything that would cause a disagreement.

That grin she'd been attracted to the minute she saw Rafe, bloomed. "Dig out a DVD and I'll make the popcorn."

Monique checked the time. It was probably too late to call Andy, and she only had the energy to be an adult with one of her relationships.

Rafe had a bigger collection of DVDs than she did. The first one she grabbed was Alfred Hitchcock's *Psycho*. It was a little too close to home. She slid it back into the pile and grabbed *It Happened One Night*. That would take her mind off everything, at least for a couple of hours.

Rafe brought a bowl of white cheddar popcorn to the coffee table and put two beers down beside it. "How was your night?"

Monique slid the DVD into the player and pressed play. She shoved a handful of popcorn into her mouth to delay responding. It couldn't hurt to tell him about Vincent coming to the club. She'd called the police, after all.

"It was interesting. I called the cops because I saw that killer in the club." She curled into his side as the movie started.

"Did they catch him?" He took a swig of his beer. His voice was relaxed, but Monique could feel his muscles tense.

"No, he got away. But I'm sure they'll get him eventually."

He grunted something that might have been agreement and then settled in to watch the movie.

Monique picked at the popcorn while she dealt with her guilt at letting Rafe believe she was letting the police handle the investigation.

"ARE YOU STAYING?" Rafe asked as the credits rolled.

Monique shook off the doze she'd fallen into about halfway through the movie. As the story unfolded, she'd started thinking about relationships. The movie couple had so much fun with all the misunderstandings, and they'd gotten over the half-truths. She didn't want that kind of relationship because in real life people didn't just laugh off lies and omissions. She needed a safe haven with Rafe, and it wasn't fair to him, or to her, to pretend things were okay when they weren't.

"I would like to stay. But we need to talk first."

He nudged her off his shoulder. "I was afraid of that. Okay tell me. I'll try to keep an open mind."

"I..." Now that she had to say it, Monique didn't know where to start.

"Let me help, Monique, please. You're still digging into the murders, right? And you don't plan to stop regardless of what I think, regardless of the danger."

She sighed, stalling so she didn't snap at him. "Yes. But it's not like that. I get that it's dangerous. I get your point. No normal person would keep pushing at this."

"So, why are you?"

He was only asking the same thing that Tess pointed out. Why didn't she want to yell at Tess the way she wanted to when Rafe asked? "I'm not normal." She tried to say it lightly, but she feared that it was the truth.

"No one is normal, Monique. What is making you put everything in jeopardy for a stranger?" He kept his voice gentle, but

Monique saw his tension in the crease on his forehead, and the tightening around his eyes.

"I've tried to work that out," Monique said. "Maybe it's because of my dad."

This time Rafe didn't bother to keep his emotion out of the words. "It's about time you got past that. It's becoming a convenient reason for everything you want to do that people, no make that me, that I don't approve of."

She sprang from the couch. "I can't believe you said that. I have tried to get over it. You just use it to point out how I'm not normal. How I don't let you in, how I don't trust anyone enough."

He watched her and it made Monique madder. She started gathering her things. This wasn't a safe haven. This was just another place where she couldn't just be herself.

He stood to face her. "Monique, don't leave. If you keep running out when we fight, we won't ever get past this."

Monique stopped what she was doing. Rafe's words touched something inside her. Did she run away? "I can't keep going over the same argument, Rafe. I leave because I don't hear anything that tells me you'll change your mind." She hoped he would hear her meaning, not just the confrontation that she couldn't keep out of the words.

Rafe looked back at her, his determination clear in the set of his jaw. "You don't give anything enough time to get to that part. If I don't agree with you right away, you leave. Will you stay this time?"

"Are you going to listen?" Everything felt as though it was balanced on a fine point. "Can we disagree and still have a relationship?"

He deflated. As though he'd just realized how big a battle he had to fight. "Yes. I don't want to stop you doing things that are important to you. At the same time, I want you safe."

Monique put down her purse and jacket. "Okay, let's talk this out. I came here to be with you tonight, Rafe, not to push you away." She sat on the other end of the couch, turning to sit with the arm at her back, crossing her legs as she faced him. "I need to know I have someone I can trust, who trusts me."

He nodded and waited for her to continue. She picked at the seam of her jeans she'd slipped on after her set, not sure where to go from there. Wasn't that enough? She realized that this was new territory for her, she'd never let someone get that important. "I guess this thing with the murders brought it home to me. I needed someone to talk to and I only had Tess. I was fighting with you, and Didi is in a coma as far as I know."

"Tess didn't strike me as someone interested in a heart to heart."

Rafe wasn't helping her, but he wasn't stopping her either. "I was lucky. The club was about to become part of the Serbian mob network. I guess I helped her out." Monique's pat response didn't feel fair to Tess. "She is not that bad, anyway."

"So how do you plan to get this done? Break the mob and catch a war criminal, without losing your life."

"I'm not sure I have a choice. I got that call. I'm pretty sure it won't be long before they realize I'm still following Vincent, if they don't already. And what if they find out I was the one who called the cops on him. After that, all they have to do is come find me, and I'm not exactly hiding."

Even under his dark skin, Monique saw him pale. She braced herself for his anger. She watched him count to ten almost aloud. A slight relaxation of the muscles in his jaw was the only indication that he was in control. "Will you stay with me, at least until this is over with?"

"I don't think fear is a good reason to move in together, Rafe. I—" she cut off the next words realizing that telling him she didn't want to move in with him at all was not the right way to keep things moving in the right direction. "I'm sorry."

"Don't panic. I'm not trying to get you in permanently, but it can't be good living across from that mess. It's going to start smelling soon." He smiled as though he'd made a joke.

"No pressure? No asking me what I'm doing?" Monique had to admit, having someone at home who would talk to her, and feed her, was tempting.

"I can't promise I won't ask, but I will do my best not to apply pressure." He gave her a real grin this time. "I might even be able to help. I do have some skills on-line."

Having Rafe do the research on the computer was a great idea. She was using him again, though. Why did it always feel like he was giving more than he was getting in the relationship? And why did that bother her when it didn't seem to bother him? "You would do that?"

"Yes, it's my way of trying to keep you out of their hands. I'll make sure that what we find on-line can't be traced. Maybe we'll be able to give the cops enough information that you won't need to go looking. And do it without committing any crimes ourselves."

Monique started to relax, just a little. They'd been talking for a half hour without a fight. "I need to go get my stuff."

Rafe rose. "I'll come with you."

"No," she snapped without thinking. Rafe drew back as if she'd hit him. "I'm sorry. I mean, I need to do this myself. You can start doing the on-line research while I'm gone. It will only take a minute for me to give you everything I know."

"Okay. If you feel like anything is wrong, you call the cops, right?"

"That's reasonable, I guess. I won't be long." She grabbed him and kissed him. "Maybe we'll fit in a little rest tonight too."

Rafe took her to the computer to gather everything she knew

about the murders. When he asked about the picture, Monique said she'd get it, and then remembered it was on her phone. She searched through the gallery and sent it to Rafe's email. "I'll be back in less than half an hour. Thanks for doing this."

"It's what people who care about each other do, Monique, they support each other." Rafe started typing search queries. "Take my keys so you don't have to buzz to get in."

Monique slipped out while he was absorbed in his work.

THE WALK HOME WAS UNEVENTFUL. The feeling of being watched was gone. Monique put it down to her stress on the way to Rafe's. She'd known they were headed for a fight. If it had been up to her, that's where it would have ended. Rafe was a good man. Maybe she should think about moving in permanently for the future if he really wanted to.

Monique ran up the stairs to her floor and opened the stair-well door. Two things hit her at once; the smell was overwhelming, and there was a man doing something to her apartment door. She put her hand out to stop the stairwell door slapping her in the face.

Her heart racing, she couldn't make a decision. She was frozen in place. Realizing she had to move forward or run away, and do it now, she still couldn't make her feet move.

Taking a deep breath made her gag. The man at her door turned at some noise, or because he'd finished.

Monique's knees buckled with relief; it was her landlord. "Bob, what are you doing here at this time of night?"

He walked toward her. "Are you okay?" He reached her and put his hand under her elbow. "I know it stinks, but it's not that bad."

She nodded and took a step forward. "I'm surprised it's taken this long for the smell to get out."

"I came by and opened the windows in there the other day. The screens are covered in bugs. It's gross and interesting at the same time. There are tons of flies in there too."

She walked to her apartment and slid her key into the lock. "Are the police finished with it?"

"Yeah, finally. That's what I was doing just now, leaving you a note. There's a crime scene clean up team coming tomorrow. The guy told me they'd be all day. They have to take out the carpet, and maybe the sub-floor. I just wanted everyone to know what was going on."

"It will be good to have it done," Monique said. "I'll be staying with my boyfriend, so I won't be bothered. When will you do the repairs?" She could stay with Rafe for more than just a couple of days, so they could fix Alexi's apartment without disturbing her. The idea didn't feel as bad as she expected, but it might give Rafe ideas.

"I haven't started figuring it out, but I need to do it soon so I can rent the place. You think people will want to rent? After two murders?"

Monique took a step into her apartment before answering, hoping Bob would take the hint. "I'm pretty sure no one will know if you don't tell them. And I won't tell anyone. You might want to ask Mac to keep his mouth shut. The rent you charge is pretty low, so you shouldn't have any problems."

"I guess. Anyway, I've got to go. My wife hates it when I work such long hours. The day job is hard enough, but I can't tell my dad I won't work in the store." He shrugged. "Anyway this should all be over in a couple of days. See you."

"Yes, take care, Bob." Monique closed her door.

She ran through her apartment gathering clothes and toiletries. She pulled the picture from its hiding place and slipped it into her purse, then grabbed a grocery bag and filled it with the fresh food from the fridge. There was no need to let that go to waste. She glanced at Didi's things and shook her head. She didn't need to drag his bags along with hers.

The conversation with Bob had slowed her down and she didn't want Rafe worrying that something had happened to her. She locked her door and ran down to the street, gulping in cold fresh air to rid herself of the taint of decay.

OUTSIDE RAFE'S BUILDING, Monique dug through her purse for his keys, feeling anxious to get inside before he worried. Her half hour had turned into almost an hour. Monique hoped he was absorbed in his work and hadn't noticed. She touched the fob against the reader and used her elbow to pull the door open.

Monique realized she was feeling something other than anxiousness for a change. She was looking forward to being with Rafe, to spending time with him. When this was over, when The Colonel was caught, maybe they could take some time off and they could get away. She could get used to this happiness thing.

The elevator opened on his floor and she missed seeing his smiling face greet her. Monique walked around the corner, sorting the keys in her fingers to bring the right one to the top. Looking up she saw that the door was unlocked and ajar. Rafe was so considerate, he'd realized she'd be handicapped with all her stuff and left the door so she just needed to push it. She bumped it open with her elbow.

"I'm sorry it took so long. Bob was there, and I had to—"

Rafe wasn't there.

Someone had been inside while she was gone. Someone who had tossed Rafe's things on the floor and tipped over the furniture. Monique let her bags drop as she ran to the small bedroom Rafe used as an office. Her heart in her throat, she pushed open the door.

The room had also been trashed, but Rafe was nowhere.

She stepped over a pile of paper that had fallen from an overturned file cabinet and inspected the desk and chair.

There was a smear of blood on the edge of the desk. Just a smear, not what she'd feared, not a pool of it with Rafe in the center carved up. The room began to spin, and she had to lower herself to the carpet, so she didn't add to the mess. She pressed her head to her knees and waited for the room to settle.

So little blood, but it had been Rafe's. She knew that without a trace of doubt. He was hurt, and he was gone.

That feeling she'd had before. Had someone followed her? How had they known which apartment was Rafe's? Was this just an unrelated random act of violence? Was it something Rafe had brought on through his work, or was it her fault?

The dizziness faded slowly. As she regained her balance, the questions in her mind focused. She knew that the odds were low that this was not related to The Colonel and the other murders. And that meant Rafe was not going to live very long. It didn't matter that she'd have to face the consequences of breaking into Alexi's apartment. She was going to tell the police everything.

It took a few more minutes for her to feel safe standing. Even then, she had to put her hand on the desk to steady herself. Her things were in the middle of the living room. Her phone was in her purse. She kept repeating the words as she made her way down the hall.

She'd call Adams' number.

She'd tell them everything.

She'd make them find Rafe, and then she'd take her punishment.

Monique stumbled into the living room and noticed a pool of milk spreading from the grocery bag. The mess brought tears. Rafe didn't need to have her making things worse. She reached for her purse and dug inside looking for her phone, regretting her penchant for black purses and black accessories. The smooth plastic slipped from her fingers twice before she was able to grasp it.

Turning it on, she blinked back the tears that blurred the screen. She was ready to redial the number when her phone rang.

Unknown number.

She slid the bar to ignore the call and tried to dial Adams' number.

The unknown caller rang again. Fucking spammers! She ignored the call again.

When the caller dialed back, she accepted it. "Look, stop calling me. I don't have time to buy whatever you are selling."

"I am not selling anything, Ms. Duchesne."

It was the same voice that had called a few days ago to warn her off. He sounded so different on the phone, but Monique knew it could only be one man. "Vincent, right?"

"Very good. At least you can remember me calling you. Too bad you didn't take my advice."

It didn't help to have confirmation that Vincent had been in the apartment. She hoped Rafe was still alive. "The police know who you are."

"Yes, that is true, but I am not afraid of your police. They are nothing like the police I know. But that is not why I called. Aren't you interested?"

Monique wasn't going to let him control the conversation. "You took Rafe."

"So direct." Vincent sighed. "Yes, we have your man."

"Is he alive?" She heard the quaver in her voice and hated him for making her sound weak.

"For now. We will see what happens."

"What do you want?" She strained to hear anything in the

background that would identify where Vincent was. There was only silence.

"You have something we want. I thought Marek took it, and you saw what I did to him, yes? And Alexi?"

"Why do you think I have it?" She was sure it was the picture, but maybe it wasn't.

"Perhaps you do not, but my friend is willing to take that chance. If you do have it, and you give it back, perhaps your man will live."

"How do I know he's still alive?" Monique picked up her purse and muted her phone so that Vincent wouldn't hear her actions. Taking the photo out, she looked around for a place to hide it. There was no reason they would come back here and look for it when she didn't hand it over. It was her only leverage, and she had to protect it. The couch cushions were lying on the floor, so she unzipped one and slid the picture between the foam and the cover. It wasn't perfect, but it would do. When that was done, she unmuted her phone and started for the door.

"Interesting, that you don't ask if you will live. You must love this man very much."

"Stop stalling, Vincent. How do I know he's alive?" She didn't ask if he was unhurt because she knew the blood was Rafe's.

"You need to show more respect. My friend will not be as amused by your spirit as I am."

"If you don't prove Rafe is alive, I'm calling the police." She locked the door before heading to the elevator.

"Calling the police will not help you, Ms. Duchesne. Your man is alive, listen."

There was a pause before Rafe mumbled through the phone. "I'm okay, Monique. Just go to the cops." The sound of something hard smashing into flesh ended with a groan.

"What do you want me to do?"

"That is a much better question. I will meet you at Lumberman's Arch. We will be alone at this time of the night, yes?"

There would be no way for her to bring help either. There
was no way to sneak up on him at that location, only one way
into Stanley Park, and only one way out.

Could she negotiate something else? "Will Rafe be there?"

"No. He will be safe here until our business is concluded."

And that meant they could kill him right now. "No. I see him,
or I go to the police with what I have."

"How do you know I don't have people waiting for you as
you leave the building?"

"Why would you just have them outside? I guess you aren't
crazy about kidnapping two people from the same building
within an hour. It might cause someone to report suspicious
behavior." She stepped out through the doors to the building.
No one came at her.

"You are on the street now."

"Yeah, you heard the elevator and the front door, no magic
there." She headed for her car. "So where am I going? The police
station? Or somewhere other than Lumberman's Arch?"

"You are right. I don't feel like going out again tonight. Come
to my office, suite 101 3500 Bleekman Street. Do not bring
anyone with you." He ended the call.

The office was only a few blocks from the catering company.
Monique fought her instincts and kept her speed just at the
limit as she drove through the almost empty streets.

18

Monique parked directly across from the building. The spot was suspiciously empty. Perhaps Vincent had arranged for it to be clear.

The building was similar to the one housing the catering company in age and construction, a big brick block with small windows. This one had no other businesses leasing space. No signs graced the front. No lights on. She wondered what they did here that would mean they needed the whole building. Then she dismissed the thought. She didn't care what happened any other time, just what was going to happen tonight.

She held her purse close to her body as she stepped from her car, not wanting to give anyone the chance to grab it, hoping it would look more like there was something of value inside.

She ran across the road and into the lobby. A single light shone through the transom of a door at the far end of the right hand corridor. The rest of the building was silent.

Monique forced herself to walk toward the light, terrified of what waited for her. The entire drive she had been imagining how she would react. She knew Vincent would kill both of them if she did something wrong, maybe even if she didn't.

If Rafe were still alive, she'd try to save him. That was the priority.

She reached out her hand to the door. It was off the latch and swung open as she touched it. The light was coming from one single bulb hanging in the center of the ceiling. It cast more shadows than light.

Taking one step inside, Monique scanned the whole room. In the far corner under a boarded up window, Rafe sat with his back against the wall, head hung low. His arm rested on his knees, something wrong with the angle of his wrist.

She took another step and whispered, "Rafe?" His head moved, not enough to look at her, but enough to indicate life. She rushed toward him trying to assess how badly he was injured. She crouched down, afraid to touch him. Bruises were forming on his face, darker swollen patches in his beautiful skin. His wrist was probably broken. As was his right ankle by the way his foot turned against the floor.

"Rafe, can you say something?" She put a finger under his chin and raised his head. He tried a grin, but it turned into a wince.

A noise behind her told Monique that her time with Rafe was done. She gave him a small nod. "It'll be okay." She rose from the crouch as she turned to face Vincent. He was alone in the room. She didn't count on that being helpful.

"Very sweet." He strode toward them slapping a leather crop against his gloved hand. "You have what I want?"

"I didn't bring it with me. You need to get him to the hospital before I tell you where it is."

He raised the crop and slashed at her in answer. Monique managed to turn so the force hit her in the shoulder. The pain immobilized her for a moment then faded. She'd be bruised but nothing felt permanently damaged. "I won't tell you anything."

"You will tell us eventually." He slapped the crop against his thigh. "Everyone talks eventually."

Monique had no doubt that he could get her to talk, but she didn't plan to let it get that far. "Yes, but you'd never know if what you want was going somewhere else while you took your time." She glanced at Rafe. "Here's how it will go. You'll call an ambulance for Rafe. You'll carry him outside – gently. You'll say you noticed him on your way by, so no one will suspect anything. And the ambulance guys won't come in here. When Rafe is on his way, I'll get the evidence I have and give it to you."

"And then I let you go?" He sneered. "I think this is too good to believe."

Monique clenched her fists to control the trembling. She couldn't let him know how frightened she really was. "What happens to me is something we'll get to. You can try it my way, or you can beat it out of me. Maybe I'll make something up to stop the pain. Maybe I've got a weak heart and I'll die before you get the information. Maybe the evidence is just waiting for the cops to find it."

Vincent smiled. It wasn't a happy sight. "This is a good plan, I am impressed. Okay we try it your way." He took out his phone and made the call to 911.

Monique bent to whisper in Rafe's ear. "You have to let him take you outside. I'll be okay. When this is over, maybe we can get away for a few days, talk about our future."

He tried to say something, but his mouth wouldn't move right. It was going to be a long road to healing. Monique blinked away the tears. She hadn't cried this much since she was eighteen. It didn't feel like it was doing any good. It felt weak and stupid.

She put her arms under Rafe's elbow and waited for Vincent to help him to his feet. Rafe was able to move while leaning on both of them to take the weight off his ankle.

Vincent started moving. "Hurry, the ambulance will not take very long. And don't try to get away. I can find him in the hospital as easily as I found him at home."

She kissed Rafe on the cheek before leaving him slumped against the wall of the building. Sirens sounded in the distance as she followed Vincent into the lobby. He continued down the hall to the office. Halfway back he seemed to realize that Monique wasn't following. He spun to face her. She waited for the punishment, but he simply smiled. "You agreed to this. Now give me the evidence."

She leaned against the wall, not willing to go anywhere until Rafe was in the ambulance, and on his way to the hospital. "No, I said when he is safe. They can't see me, don't worry."

He moved to stand beside her. His silent presence almost as frightening as his threats. Monique felt her body contract, as if she could make herself small enough to avoid his attention. That wasn't going to give her the edge she needed. Acting and looking like a victim wouldn't save her life. Shifting subtly, she expanded until she was standing up straight.

The lights from the ambulance flooded the hallway as it stopped in front of the doors. Vincent took her arm in a painful grip and pulled her farther into the hall. She tried to shrug him off, but he squeezed harder until she gasped with the pain. "Just a taste. Now it is time for your part. Where is the evidence?"

The pain was intense, Monique had to hiss her words out, "If you don't let me go, I'll scream, and that will bring everyone in. You know they send the cops with the ambulance, right?" She had no idea if that was true.

"In the office. Now." He pulled her so fast she couldn't cry out.

When they were inside, Vincent closed the door with a gentleness that frightened her. He was tightly in control, and she needed him to get angry enough to be careless.

She pushed away the pain in her arm. "What is the big deal, Vincent? Why is this evidence so important?"

He flung her across the room. "Where is it?" His voice was still calm and quiet. The violence of his actions contrasted with his voice, brought a shiver of terror to Monique.

She sent the fear into the place where she kept the horror of her father's actions. Into a dark part of herself that could contain all the fear in her life. "Do you even know what it is? Doesn't he trust you enough to tell you?"

That struck home, she saw a flicker of something hot and resentful. "I do not need to know anything more than I am told. You have something that can harm the man I work for. Something I need to get from you." He slid his fingers around her neck and squeezed enough to make her choke. Then, when he saw her understand how close she was to death, he raised his other fist. "If you survive, you do want to continue to sing, yes? I can make it impossible. I can make your voice broken."

Monique blinked unable to speak. She waited for his fist to land, to feel her cheek shatter. Instead he lowered his fist and released her throat. She wheezed in a breath that started a coughing fit. Vincent waited patiently for her to get control, that creepy smile across his lips the whole time.

She finally got control of her breathing and along with the rush of oxygen came a plan to survive. "How will you know whether it's the right thing?"

"I don't have to know that. You will wait until it is verified. Then we will decide what to do with you." He dragged her to the door. "Now you will take me to it."

Monique pulled her arm out of his grip and rubbed away the pain. "Okay, relax. We can go. I'll drive."

"No, I will drive. You will give me directions." He shoved her through the door. When they were on the street, Vincent kept dragging her by the arm until they reached a black SUV. He unlocked the door and pushed her into the seat. "Do I have to lock you to the door?"

"No, I'll behave." She wasn't going to get away here, besides there was nowhere to run.

Vincent slammed the door and walked around, keeping his eyes on her the whole time he was outside. When he was settled into the driver's seat, he glanced at her. "Buckle up, it's safer." He curled his lip in a smile. "I would hate to be pulled over because you violate the seatbelt law, yes?"

Monique clicked the seatbelt closed.

He waited. "Do I have to beat you to get the directions? I can, but it's difficult while we sit in the car."

Monique shook her head. "Go to Gastown. I hid it in one of the tourist shops. I have a key." He knew she worked at A Walk in The Past, so it would add some credibility to the story.

"Don't try anything. If I kill you, perhaps that will be enough. Perhaps this evidence will be lost." He started the car.

Monique looked out for police cruisers as they drove, none were about. And no one was coming to rescue her. Rafe wouldn't be able to tell anyone what happened until something was done about his jaw. "Where do you come from, Vincent?"

"Why do you want to know? Getting to know me is not going to save your life. I know these tricks. I have used them to my advantage." He sped up to make an amber light.

"It will pass the time. It gives me something to think about." *And something to keep you occupied while I figure out a way to escape.*

"I am from Yugoslavia."

"Which part?"

He glanced at her. "When I left it was no sides. Just Yugoslavia."

That seemed odd, ten years since the war and he wasn't taking sides? "You have family there?"

His mouth tightened. "No. They died in the war. I do not wish to speak of this again. Where am I going?"

Why was he working for a war criminal? Maybe he didn't know. That was a dangerous game for The Colonel to play. "Park on Water Street near Main. We won't get any closer at this time of night, there will be too many cabs waiting for the clubs to close."

They parked and Vincent grabbed her arm, walking close enough that people would think they were together. His grip was tight but not enough to hurt.

"Where?"

Monique nodded toward the closest alley. One she knew well from her tours, one that turned a dogleg and opened out onto Hastings where she could run.

Vincent gave her a shove. "Give me the key."

"I have to do it. I have to reach inside and put in the code before the alarm goes off." She wriggled her arm. "I need both hands."

He looked around. There were voices coming from down the street. Drunks returning home to the gentrified parts of the neighborhood. He pushed her a little farther down the alley until the drunks passed, then returned her to the door. Monique didn't react to the fact he'd missed where the alley turned.

"No tricks." He let her arm go.

Monique pretended to fumble in her pocket for keys, hoping the crowds would come closer. She only needed Vincent to be distracted for a second.

"Hurry," he snapped.

"Hey man, what's going on?" One of the passing drunks called out.

Vincent turned to order them away. Monique ran toward the end of the alley around the dumpster, and through the gloom toward the streetlights and noise of Hastings Street. The sound of Vincent running behind, drove her to a breakneck speed. She ignored the feeling that he was just about to grab her shoulder. Monique just ran. Her focus on the sounds of traffic and people ahead.

On Hastings, no matter the time, there were always people hanging around. The drug trade didn't keep regular hours. Vincent wouldn't want too many witnesses. And she could find a cop, or something. If she could find a few seconds safe and alone, she could call Adams.

She turned right as soon as she hit Hastings, running toward the corner of Main where she saw two uniformed cops talking to a group of women who were obviously lost. If she could get their attention, she'd be safe, if only for a little while.

Vincent's steps stopped pounding after her. She didn't look to see if he had stopped or just slowed to a walk. She kept running toward the cops who were getting into their cruiser and leaving. Her heart stopped. She looked around and saw Vincent on the phone, probably calling for reinforcements. Or was he ordering someone to go hurt Rafe?

She spun in place, suddenly unsure of where to go.

If she ran south, there would be fewer crowds to hide in. If she went north the police station was only three blocks away, but Vincent could catch her before she was safe.

Now she couldn't stop looking at Vincent. He stared back and pointed a finger as though it was a gun. It chilled her and she slowed her dash before she realized it.

Vincent started forward stalking her like a lion on a wounded gazelle.

Why didn't anyone notice what was going on. She started walking backward in the direction of the police station. It was her only hope. Vincent sped up and Monique stopped watching him and just ran.

There were still enough people around to keep him from

just shooting her. Monique knew that the leather crop was in his jacket. She was sure he had a gun as well. If he decided to cut his losses, then she was going to be dead as soon as he followed her around the corner.

She sped up and turned the corner. Another alley beckoned.

She had a chance. If she could get into the alley before Vincent came around the corner, she'd be hidden behind a dumpster and dialing Adams' number.

She hurled herself around the corner and halfway down it to the first dumpster. The stench was overwhelming, but she closed her mouth and hunkered down. Reaching for her phone, she turned it on then immediately turned it off before anyone saw the light. Her plan was not going to work. Vincent would be looking through the alley any second.

Behind her was a rusty door. Without much hope, she slid her fingers through the handle and tugged. It opened a few inches. She pulled again thankful that there was no light behind it. Despite the condition of the door, it swung quietly. She slipped inside, pulling it shut behind her. Using her phone for light, she saw a lock and turned it. Vincent wouldn't be able to tell she had gone in.

An unlocked door in this neighborhood didn't bode well, but there was nothing inside this building that could be worse than Vincent. She followed the hall to the end where a short flight of concrete steps led to another open door.

The screen gave light but showed her there were no bars. So no call to Adams, but at least she could hole up for a while. A little luck and higher up there might be a window where she could find service. Monique figured she had some good luck owed to her.

She made her way up three flights of stairs before she heard voices. A line of people filled the hall, all of them agitated, some twitching, and some scratching at their skin as though trying to remove something underneath.

"Get in line, bitch," one of the women snapped as Monique tried to get past the crowd. "They are packaging right now."

Junkies waiting for a fix. There would be nothing else in the building if a meth lab was operating. That might be a good thing. If the rest of the building was empty, she would be able to find a place to hide.

Monique stepped away from the line-up and tried to find another way out of the building. The front door was boarded up and so were all the windows facing the street – and still no bars on her phone.

She realized that the alley was her only choice for an exit, and she had no idea if Vincent would still be looking for her there. Regardless, she needed to get to somewhere she could call for help. It was only a matter of time before Vincent, or one of his friends, decided to get to Rafe and hurt him.

She worked her way back to the basement door, heart trying to climb out of her chest. Voices came from the top of the stairs. It would be helpful if she could go out with one of the junkies. If Vincent were there, he wouldn't be looking for her as part of a group. Could she afford to wait for an escort?

The voices came closer and Monique could make out a few words. It was at least two men. Perhaps they weren't junkies. Perhaps they were dealers, which would make it more difficult to just follow them. There was no way they'd miss her, and, in all probability, they'd think she was trying to steal from them. It didn't matter at this point. She was going to follow them and hope for the best. She stepped into the shadow of a doorway.

"Yeah, that corner is good earlier, but at this time there's no traffic." The short, skinny one was doing the talking. He was wearing a heavy jacket with a New York Yankee's crest.

"I'm heading home," the other man said. This one was

heavier and taller, same jacket. "I have to be home to take Vanessa to school tomorrow."

They passed Monique without noticing her. As soon as they were a foot in front of her, she uncurled from the shadow and followed.

Even though she stepped quietly, the two men noticed her. That must be some kind of drug dealer's survival response. They looked her up and down, then turned away. Monique wasn't sure if she was happy that her pretense of being a junkie worked, or annoyed that they didn't see her as a threat. She decided on being pleased, because she had no need to be a threat to anyone.

The two men cleared the alley and Monique paused before stepping into the street. There were very few people about, but a block away, she saw the lights of the police station. And in the opposite direction the activity on Hastings Street. If she turned left it was a clear run to safety, but no cover if Vincent was somewhere between her and the door.

To the right, the dubious cover of crowds where she could make a call. She turned on her cell phone. There was one bar, maybe the call would go through if the sliver of green on her battery was enough to power it.

Monique figured her chances were better in a one-block run. Vincent wouldn't be stupid enough to try to shoot her so close to the police station. At least, that's what she told herself.

A quick glance around and she pushed off from the alley.

No one was in sight between her and the light of the station. There were a few shadowed doorways, but none big enough to hide Vincent.

It didn't matter who was on duty. A woman afraid of being killed would get their attention enough for her to tell the whole story.

And she would. No more holding back on anything she'd done. No more—

She was yanked off her feet and pulled into one of the shadowed doorways. It was the entrance to an empty community center. Deeper than a shop door. Deep enough to hold Vincent and another man.

Monique kicked and scratched, but she couldn't cry out through the hand across her mouth.

"You should not have run away," Vincent breathed into her ear. "Now you will be punished for that. We will have some fun, and you will give us the evidence."

The other man said something that Monique couldn't make out through her struggles. And then Vincent slapped tape over her mouth and tied her hands. "I can knock you out, or you can wait quietly here with this man until I bring the car. You choose."

Monique's only hope was to remain conscious, so she could take any opportunity to escape. She went limp in his hands. "Good little girl. Now, no trouble. My friend has a knife. He is very skilled. He has learned where to cut to make the most pain without killing."

She nodded and let him place her in the dark corner like a bag of trash.

While Vincent brought the car, Monique tried to identify the man who was waiting with her. It was too dark to see any features, but he was tall, well over six feet, and thin. He didn't say anything, just stood there facing her. She could almost feel the tension in his body.

Was he just waiting for an excuse to hurt her? Was he going to do something just because he could?

He had ordered Vincent around, so he must be high in the organization. Maybe The Colonel himself? She didn't think that could be right. Why would The Colonel get involved here on the street? Why risk exposing himself? The only reason would be that he knew what Alexi had, and that no one in his organization knew who he really was.

If that were true, then The Colonel would be afraid she'd say something that would tip people off. And perhaps he would have to fear retribution from his own men. Men whose families he'd tortured or wiped out.

No wonder he'd told Vincent to gag her.

If she had guessed right, how was he going to get her to tell them where the picture was without taking the chance she'd blurt out what she knew?

As soon as the gag came off, as soon as she knew for sure who this man was, Monique vowed she would tell Vincent everything.

19

V incent pulled the SUV up to the curb. Monique struggled against the man who hoisted her into the back seat and pushed her onto the floor. They made sure she had no chance of catching the interest of other drivers by showing her duct-taped mouth. She prayed they wouldn't hit any speed bumps or make any sudden stops, because there was no place to brace herself, and no padding if she did bang into something. At least Vincent pulled away from the curb smoothly. Monique was sure it was to keep the cops from getting interested, not for her comfort.

She tried to keep track of where they were going by the motion of the SUV as it turned corners. Three turns into the journey and she was lost, only a vague notion that they were traveling east remained. She suspected they would make sure she couldn't see her location when they stopped.

Monique didn't know what she could do to improve her chances of living, but she realized that she didn't want to die with so many empty places in her life. She needed time to fix things with Rafe, and Didi. Maybe time to build more relationships and fewer walls.

The vehicle rolled to a stop after what felt like a half hour to Monique, but it could have been anything from five minutes to an hour. The only thing she could verify was that it was still dark, so it was no later than four a.m.

The two men spoke in a language Monique couldn't understand. Then Vincent wrapped something around her eyes before lifting her out of the SUV.

He placed Monique on her feet and used her tied hands to steer her. Nothing was said the whole time. Monique didn't know if that was intentional or not. She did know it made her feel like an object. Is that how they make it easy to torture and kill? By taking the humanity out of their victims?

She did her best to follow the directions Vincent communicated through pulls and pushes on her arms. Because she'd been tied up so tightly, the pain of the smallest movement ripped through her shoulders and down her arms, running like fire to her fingertips. It was hard to concentrate on her surroundings to get clues. She could hardly breathe with the agony of every little movement.

She stumbled up three steps and then the feeling of the wind on her skin stopped, and the ambient sounds of traffic ended. The silence only added to her terror. When they uncovered her eyes, if they were planning to do that, what would she see?

Some kind of slaughterhouse?

Some kind of torture room?

A final push from Vincent and she pitched into a wall, almost blacking out at the searing pain that ran through her body. Monique slid down the wall to a sitting position, back braced against it, waiting for their next move.

The sound of a chair scraping across a gritty floor broke the silence. A soft voice uttered words in the same language they'd been speaking earlier. Then she felt a tug at the blindfold and light shocked her into squeezing her eyes shut.

"Open your eyes," the man who might be The Colonel said. His voice was soft as though speaking to a frightened child. When she obeyed, Monique looked up to see him sitting in the chair, right leg crossed over his left at the knee.

She stared into deadest eyes she'd ever seen. The man looked even thinner now that he had shed the heavy coat. His face was pale and pockmarked. His hair dyed that impossible black that men thought looked natural and scraped back with some kind of sculpting product.

He smiled and she saw a gap where he was missing a tooth. "Vincent will take off your gag. You will not scream?" He said it as if she could choose what to do, but Monique knew it was an order not a question.

She nodded and braced herself for more pain. Vincent lifted a corner of the tape and slowly peeled it away, hardly hurting her at all.

"Now, Ms. Duchesne, I have some questions and you will answer them."

It looked like Vincent was going to be silent through this. Monique wondered what he would do if she told him who this man was? She could see the resemblance to the mug shot online. He'd had something done to his jaw and nose, but not enough to fool anyone who knew his identity. Maybe it would have worked better if he'd done something with his skin, but then he might not have been able to take any more cosmetic surgery on such bad pockmarks.

"You know who I am?"

That was a loaded question. Monique decided he meant his current identity. Now that she was in a position to tell Vincent, she found she couldn't. What made her think Vincent would react like a normal person? Maybe he knew and didn't care. Maybe psychopaths didn't do revenge. "No, but I guess you are a big shot in the local gangs."

"I am. My name is Ivan Novikov."

So she'd guessed right about his cover story. Still unsure of Vincent's reaction, she didn't respond.

Before Ivan/Javor could ask his next question, Monique's phone rang. He pointed at her purse and Vincent dug out her phone, turning the display to his boss.

"Who is this person, Andy?" Ivan asked.

"A friend. He's a doctor."

"Then I think we will answer, yes? You will only say hello."

He hit the bar to answer and Monique did as she was told.

"Nique? Don't get mad."

Didi. She felt a wave of relief that he was awake and alive. She opened her mouth to say she was busy despite Ivan's stare.

"Let me talk, Nique. It's important I get this out. Part of the treatment, you know. I'm sorry I've been such a shitty brother. It wasn't fair of me to leave you to handle all the problems on your own. Look, I'm going to be here for a day more, if you have time, come see me, please. I want to start making things right. I'm in the River March Clinic, room ten. Bye."

Just like Didi. He never thought that she might have something to say. Now they knew she had a brother. And worse, they knew where to find him.

"Turn off the phone. We don't need to be interrupted again." Ivan returned his attention to her. "Your brother will be safe as long as you do as I tell you, your brother, and your lover."

Monique waited for him to ask for the evidence. She would tell him it was at Rafe's. She'd tell him how to find it, and anything else he wanted to know. Whatever kept Didi and Rafe safe.

"You think I will let you walk away from here?"

She licked her lips, wondering if he expected a response.

"I have given many people reason to regret crossing me. It is no longer just about what you took. Now I need to provide a lesson to some people who I believe may be talking to the police about my activities. People I trusted, perhaps foolishly."

Vincent moved to lean against the wall beside her. When Ivan spoke, Vincent shifted and reached for his leather crop.

Monique twisted her wrists against the plastic zip strip that held them together. All that did was hurt and cut her wrists enough for blood to ooze. The warm sticky liquid dribbling down her hand to her fingers.

"So you don't want the thing I took?" If she could stall him, maybe something would happen that she could use to escape. If not, the longer she put off the start of his fun, the better.

"Yes, we will get to that soon. I want you to understand what will happen to you. To get you in the mood." He reached into his pocket making her tense in preparation for pain. He pulled out a pack of cigarettes and gold lighter. The scent of burning tobacco started her heart racing. He smiled as though he knew what was happening to her.

She licked her lips again. "Do you hurt people a lot? Is that what business you are in?"

He cocked his head at Vincent. "You can leave us."

Glancing at her, Vincent looked like he smelled something foul. "I'll wait outside. When you are ready, just call."

When they were alone, Ivan stubbed out his cigarette on the floor, and then rose to stand over her. "You know who I really am. That fool Alexi told me he had proof of my previous identity."

"Yes. I found you on-line. You are Colonel Javor Dragic. You're wanted by the war crimes tribunal." Twisting her wrists still wasn't doing anything to release them. If she could get free, she'd have a fighting chance.

"Did you read my history? Was that available on-line?" He sounded proud of his accomplishments.

She hadn't been interested in the details, trusting that a war criminal had committed atrocities that she didn't need to understand. "I don't know if the details were there." As much as she didn't need to hear what he'd done, keeping him talking might mean he wouldn't start the torture.

"I have killed hundreds of people. Some say thousands. That is what they know I did. I tortured many others. People they will never find."

Monique tuned out the words, using the time to think about how to get out of the zip ties. She remembered reading something about their design when she had used them to put up her Christmas lights.

Yes, they were designed to open when you did something to the lock. She stopped twisting and started feeling as much as she could with her fingers. She touched the bulk of the locking mechanism and felt the tongue that caught on the ridges.

She just needed to push that and the tie would unzip.

She let her focus go back to Ivan, or Javor. She needed to make sure she wasn't ignoring his questions while she unzipped her bound hands.

He wasn't paying attention to her. He was standing, looking inside a black bag that sat open on the seat of the chair. Then he spoke in that calm voice, "I have cut the fingers off people as they watched, as their children watched. I find that wire cutters are the best for that." He turned and held up a pair of rusty wire cutters.

Monique swallowed the bile that rose at the image of him snipping her fingers off.

She managed to unzip a few more ridges.

"So many people think that torture doesn't work. They say the victim will confess to anything to end the pain and fear. What do you think?"

Monique froze. She hadn't anticipated having to take part in the conversation. "I tend to agree with them." She watched as Ivan walked toward her with the wire cutters ready to use. The cutting edges opening and closing like a hungry mouth.

"Do you ever wonder why it is so popular if that is true? Why it continues to be used for all these centuries?" He held the cutters up to her face. When she flinched, he laughed. His breath was sour. "No answer? So, you understand how it begins. How the fear starts to build." He walked back to the bag.

Monique worked the zip ties rapidly while his back was turned, stopping only as he spun to face her.

The ties were almost loose enough.

"There's a secret to successful torture." He pulled out a long probe then tossed it back in the bag, but not before Monique saw it was stained with old blood. "It's about balance. Too much will make your victim say anything, and too little will not elicit any information. I prefer to help people understand what is the right action. The action that will save their loved ones, even if not themselves."

It was getting harder for Monique to control the zip strip. There was enough slack for the lock to slip out of her fingers. She needed to concentrate enough to slide it, so she could hold it in one hand and use the other to unzip. Every time she moved it, it snapped out of her fingers, and she lost track of where the lock was.

"Who are your loved ones, Ms. Duchesne? Is it just your junkie brother and your black lover?"

Slowly moving the zip strip through her fingers, Monique concentrated on not letting it bounce away from her grip. "I don't gather friends. I don't really care about people." The lock touched her right hand. She shifted it carefully so she could stick her finger into the mechanism. With all this straining, her muscles were going to hurt even more tomorrow – if she was alive to feel anything.

Ivan stopped digging through the bag and glanced at her over his shoulder. Monique realized that from his point of view, the torture had begun, and he was enjoying her reaction.

Sure, she was scared, but not enough to betray anyone, yet. Was she just stupid? Or was it because she didn't live in a world of terror? His other victims would be living with the fear of knowing what was coming. She could only imagine it. They would have been living with the fear of meeting this fate for far longer than a few days.

"You can avoid all this pain if you tell me where the evidence is. I promise that you will stop feeling pain when I have what I need."

Monique didn't believe him. He meant he would stop the torture. She was going to die unless she could get out of here. "Do the others know who you are?"

He smiled. "No, and if they did, it would probably be a very bad thing for me. I am not the man I was in the war. I am now more interested in the money than the ideology. Perhaps they will not forgive me, and then again, perhaps they will."

The zip tie was almost loose enough to let Monique slip her hands free. All she needed was an opportunity to use the freedom it would give her. She needed some advantage, something that would get her out of the door and to a phone. Monique had no illusions about how long she would be able to stay out of their grasp, or about how an accusation against Ivan would affect Vincent. No matter what Ivan had done, Vincent would never be her ally.

"How long do you think it will be before someone recognizes you? If I can see through the plastic surgery you've had done, others will." She held the ends of the zip tie between her fingers. It had to look like she was still under his control or she'd lose the advantage.

"They look for what they want to see. And they want to forget the war. Believe me, there is no future in keeping the past alive. No matter who was killed, or who won, they are sheep and want to get on with their petty lives." He pulled a chisel out of the bag. "This does a good job of breaking joints."

"If you kill me, how will you get the evidence? You don't know what it is." She felt cold sweat starting in the small of her back. She only had a little time before Ivan would start acting on all these threats.

"It is something that you used to recognize me. It is something that Alexi used to blackmail me. If he was able to find out the truth, this must be a simple piece of evidence. Alexi was good at bringing in credit cards, but he was... how do you say? Oh, yes, not the brightest bulb in the package."

"Close enough. You're right. I did hide it. How will you retrieve it without giving yourself away?" The memory of sending the photo to Rafe floated though the fear and pain. She could tell them where the picture was and maybe they wouldn't realize she had a copy. One that would prove who Ivan really was easier than the original.

"That is a very good question. I cannot trust anyone, this is true. I will have to retrieve it for myself." He flung the chisel with a twist of his wrist. It landed blade down in the floor two inches from Monique's left foot.

It happened so quickly, she didn't have time to react and give herself away. The zip tie was still firmly grasped in her fingers.

"So, you'll leave me here with Vincent while you get it?" That would give her a chance to put doubt in Vincent's mind.

"I will ensure you cannot speak to him, do not worry. I have in here more than just crude tools. I have something that will make you unconscious for enough time."

Monique swallowed the fear that she would lose her only chance to get away. "And then?"

"You are a very curious young lady," he said, a touch of admiration in his voice. "If you are telling the truth, I will give him instructions to kill you quickly. If you are not, perhaps burning to death in the unfortunate fire that destroys this building would make up for your lies."

Monique knew she couldn't let The Colonel leave, because as soon as he was on his way to get the picture, Victor would be ending her life painfully. "If I lie then you kill me. If I tell the truth, you kill me. Painful or not, I'm still dead. I need more incentive."

He sat on the chair again. "So, a negotiation. Well, I have some time. Tell me what you propose to offer me to save your life."

"What do I have to negotiate with?" Monique continued the conversation so she could run contingency plans through her mind. The only weapon within reach was the chisel. If she went for that and couldn't get it out of the floor, she'd be dead, or worse.

"Your brother. Your lover. What would you do to keep them safe?"

She tried not to stare at the chisel while she thought about her answer. "How do I know you'll keep any deal we make? I'll be dead after all."

He checked his nails while he thought about his answer. Monique wasn't sure that his coolness was fake. He seemed to lack any of the emotions that he was trying to build in her. In fact, despite his efforts to build her fear, he wasn't reacting to it at all. "I suppose my word will not be enough to reassure you?"

"No, unless you plan to keep me around to check on you."

She slid her leg forward as though she was getting a cramp. The chisel was within reach of her foot. If she wasn't too stiff, she could drop the zip ties and lunge. Could she grab it and stab him in one move?

"That might be possible." His words echoed eerily with Monique's internal dialogue. "We have places we could hold you indefinitely. I have men who would enjoy your company for a price, at least for a while."

She couldn't know for sure if the chisel would work. Sitting in one position could have frozen her muscles. She wouldn't know until she tried to move. "I'm no prostitute. They might not like it."

"These men would enjoy a fight." He held up a finger for Monique to wait and pulled his phone out of his pocket, an old model. "Bok?" The conversation continued in a foreign language. It seemed to be comprised of short questions and answers. Ivan kept his eyes on Monique as he spoke, leaving her no opportunity to attack.

She let a look of pain cross her face and jerked her leg. The chisel stopped her foot before popping out of the floor. It landed just beyond her reach. Ivan seemed to have bought the charley horse act because he didn't react. The chisel was still in play, if she could get to it, and act fast enough.

The call ended and Ivan placed the phone on the table before turning his attention back to her. "So, are you willing to tell me where this evidence is? I have another... meeting to attend."

"It's a picture of you before. When you were a war criminal. Or, I guess, when you were being one. You still are a war criminal."

That seemed to surprise him. "There are no pictures of me."

"How do you know that?"

"I was careful. I did not wish there to be any repercussions from my... service in the name of my country."

"You knew you'd need to hide your identity all along."

"Yes, I am not a stupid man. So, one photograph survived."

Monique flexed her muscles, trying to test her chance of getting off the floor fast. "Two pictures. There's the one I have, and the mug shot on the war criminal site."

"That one I don't worry about. It was taken after I had been beaten by the men who caught me. I think they applied makeup to cover the damage. I should have thanked them before killing them. They made it possible for me to hide. That is the only official picture of me."

"True, I found it hard to see the comparison at first."

"The surgeon assured me that no one would be able to recognize me."

"You need to go back to him and get a refund." Monique tensed and released her muscles to bring life back to them.

"That is not possible. He is retired – permanently."

Monique cocked her head. "Too bad, you could have used him again. It didn't take a lot for me to see the similarity. If someone suspects who you are, they'll see the proof." She shifted on her hip to make sure she would be able to lever herself up. Pins and needles ripped through her body then ebbed. "Why don't we invite Vincent in to see if he sees what I do?"

"You are amusing. Perhaps I will keep you alive to continue that. Like a monkey who will dance on a leash."

She leaned back and placed the zip tie on the ground, bracing her hands on the floor. "I'm not a good pet." She tried to put all her hatred into the words. Not just the hatred of Ivan, and what he had done, but hatred of her father and his actions, of the people who sold Didi drugs, of anyone who tried to change her.

"You will learn." He took the bag and dug around in it again, pulling out a leather rope. "This will look good wrapped around your neck."

She stared at it. Two lengths of black and brown leather straps braided into a four-foot long rope. "Not my color."

"I sense you think you can win here, Ms. Duchesne. You must know what I am capable of. Why do you hesitate to tell me exactly what I need to know?" On the table beside the leather strap went a syringe and a small bottle, then a straight razor.

"Do you think that violence is inherited?" she asked the question casually. "What were your parents like?"

He raised an eyebrow. Clearly, he hadn't expected to get anything other than an answer to his question. "They were farmers. They liked being farmers. They didn't understand wanting more. I don't see what this has to do with the picture you have."

"Do you wonder how you came by your... talents? Were you adopted?"

"No. I have never questioned anything. I am the product of my ambitions. Now you have intrigued me. Why do you ask this question? Are you adopted?" He sat on the chair to wait for her answer.

"I have hoped I was. That is, I hoped it since I was eighteen. I believe in genetics having an effect on behavior."

He nodded for her to continue.

Monique wasn't sure how to do that. She hadn't realized how true that statement was, and it shocked her to know she wanted to throw away the love and support she'd received for eighteen years because of one incident that didn't make any sense.

An incident she still secretly thought wasn't her father's action. Her father couldn't have done what the police said he'd done. It was so far away from the man she knew that it didn't make any sense to her.

Ivan was relaxed and Monique's pins and needles had subsided. This was the time to move, if she was going to do it. The realization shortened her breath and the room seemed to dim, her focus only on Ivan, the chair he was sitting in, and the chisel.

She would need to rotate on her hip, sweep her hand to the chisel and stand in one motion. She would need to have her hand at Ivan's throat before he could react and either attack her or call for Vincent.

20

M onique realized she hadn't been rehearsing when she felt Ivan's shoulder under her right hand while her left hand held the chisel to his throat.

She had no memory of moving.

The chisel sat against Ivan's Adam's apple. If he tried to call for Vincent, she could shove it through his neck before the sound came out.

He wasn't worried. A smile curled his lips and the muscles under her hand were relaxed. If she didn't want to kill him, she would have to convince him that she could. Thankfully, she didn't have to convince herself. If it came down to it, she'd kill him as easily as she'd slap a mosquito. Whatever the consequences, she'd deal with them later.

"You cry out and I'll jam this into your throat." The words ground out through clenched teeth, but they had no effect on Ivan.

Monique glanced into the bag and saw duct tape. Restraining him was now a real option. But she needed to make sure he wouldn't try anything while she reached for the tape.

She believed that her reluctance to speak about her father

all these years had kept her sane. The counselor had tried to get her to open up, saying it would help her heal, but she'd never believed it. Whether it helped her or not, it would work to show Ivan she might be capable of killing him.

"You haven't had a chance to research me like I have you. If you had, you would know what my family is capable of." It wasn't easy to say what she needed to say, but she kept talking, "My brother hid in drugs. I hid in denial, but I know what my father did is something I could do. I don't know why he did it, but I'll do it to protect people I love. Do you want to know what he did? Oh, yeah, you can't talk. Just blink once."

Ivan blinked. Monique pushed aside her nausea to keep speaking, "He loved me and my brother very much. I thought he loved my mother too, but it turned out he didn't. When I came home one day, I found out what he was capable of. I found out that he could kill my mother without any apparent reason. That he could stick a knife in her over and over again. The coroner said he started with her throat so she couldn't cry out. Maybe I should do that to you?"

Monique took a breath and noticed Ivan was sweating. So, he was susceptible to the same tactics as he used on others. She smiled down at him and drew back the hand holding the chisel slightly. There was a line of blood oozing just below his Adam's apple. Monique experienced no feeling of panic this time. "At least that part I understand. Now, how does it feel to be on the other side of this?"

She pulled the chisel away again, just far enough to let him speak.

"It is interesting. I will take a lesson away from this, if I am allowed to take anything away. But I wonder are you really willing to take a life? It changes you. The first kill is the hardest one. You have no understanding of the pleasure you receive when the life drains out of your victim. After that, you can anticipate it. I remember a man, a boy really, who used to stab women. He was my role model, the one who helped me realize my power."

"I don't care." Monique shifted the chisel again.

Ivan swallowed. "Maybe you should care, but it doesn't matter. I lost contact with him when he came to this country. More than thirty years ago. He had your eyes."

Monique felt all her blood sink to her stomach, leaving her head and fingers cold. This man was talking about her father. Was it the truth? Was he trying to rattle her?

Had her father been a killer before... No, she wouldn't believe Ivan's lies. "I hope killing for a good reason is different. I think I'll get away with it legally, and I've lived with the emotional fallout of violence long enough that I think I can deal with it. Maybe I need to change, maybe it will be good."

"Perhaps you will be different from me. I also first killed to protect someone I loved."

"I find it hard to believe you understand love. I think you tell yourself that, but you like it. I saw it in your eyes. You got off on the fear. You hate it when someone dies because it means you can't terrorize them any longer." Whether it was true or not, Monique kept talking.

She moved behind Ivan before reaching for the tape. Using her teeth, Monique pulled off a length, then slapped it over his mouth. She taped him to the chair and picked up the phone.

Flipping it open, Monique dialed 911.

Nothing happened.

She looked at the status. There were no bars.

What the hell kind of night was it? She would have to get outside to make the call and Vincent was in the hall. She'd used up all the energy she had to play the dangerous killer. A quick glance at the windows showed her the security mesh. There was no other way out of the room. She looked at Ivan. He stared back at her, fury burning in his gaze. She shivered but didn't respond to the unspoken threat.

Moving to the window, she tried the phone again, only one bar. Ivan was rocking the chair. She knew it would break if he could manage to get enough momentum to fall. Running to stop him, she looked for something that would at least slow him down. The drug was unfamiliar, but she could tell by the way his eyes widened that it wasn't just a truth serum. She wasn't going to take a chance on the dosage. She needed to find something that would help her without risking killing him. He was right about that. Despite her earlier confidence, she didn't want to take the chance that it would change her for the worst.

The only thing that came to her mind was to lower the chair to the floor so he couldn't break it with a fall. She took the back of the chair in her hands and braced herself. Ivan tried to rock, but she tipped the chair back giving him nothing to push against. His weight made it difficult to handle, but she slowly lowered him to the ground. On his back, he had less ability to move. Monique knew it wouldn't be long before he was able to change that.

Simply making the phone call wouldn't protect her life. If he got free, she would be dead before the cops could arrest him. Monique needed to get outside. She tested both windows with no luck. The only way out was past Vincent.

If she could get him to come in, perhaps she could slip out. If she ran fast, there were places she could hide for long enough to be safe. Too many ifs for comfort, but she had no choice.

First, she needed to hide Ivan so that Vincent would be distracted. Then she needed to get Vincent's attention. The only way that would work is if she broke something, loudly.

It needed to be something fast. If she delayed much longer, Vincent might just come in to find out what was taking so long.

The only thing in the room that would hide Ivan for even a

moment was the table. If she pulled it to stand beside him, and placed the bag on the floor, it might work. She lifted the table to his side, and took a moment to tape Ivan's feet together, further limiting his ability. He was trying to yell at her through the tape and it came out as a grunting wheeze.

"Feeling some sympathy for your victims? Or are you beyond that? Don't bother trying to answer. I'm sure you don't want me to demonstrate anything else about their experience."

She went to the door and looked. Unless Vincent's height gave him more of an advantage than she imagined, the first glance would show him a table and bag. That's all she needed, just a few seconds of distraction.

Now she had to figure out how to break something noisily and do it from her position at the door. She had to be standing in the corner beside the door as soon as Vincent entered. He wouldn't see her right away – if she were very lucky.

The window was the most likely target, but she didn't think she could throw hard enough, or accurately enough, to break the glass through the bars. What else would make enough noise? She went back to the bag. Maybe she didn't have to break anything. Maybe there was another way. There was a hammer. She could use that to bang on the door. The leather rope gave her an idea. She looked at the radiator near the door.

She tied one end of the rope to the radiator about two inches from the floor. Then she trailed the rope across the opening and held onto the other end. Finally, she banged on the door, enjoying the loud crashing as a release of the tension she'd been holding so close.

There was no sound of approach, but she kept her eyes on the door handle.

It turned.

The door opened outward.

She waited until Vincent took his first step inside then

pulled the rope tight. It caught him halfway up his shin and he pitched forward. She let the rope go and rushed through the doorway as Vincent hit the ground with a thud and groan.

The hall was empty.

It had occurred to her that Vincent might have brought reinforcements while he waited, but no. Behind her, she heard cursing and furniture breaking. Monique kept running.

Taking a left outside the door, she ran toward the end of the street dodging between two cars so she could run behind the parked vehicles as cover. She flipped open the phone and pressed 911.

"Police," she gasped out to the operator as she glanced at the street signs. "I'm on Arles Avenue and Pandora. I need the police. Someone is trying to kill me. Hurry!"

She heard a shout behind her, but it didn't seem directed, just frustrated.

"Ma'am stay on the line, the police are on the way."

Monique hazarded a glance and saw Vincent in the doorway looking up and down the street. She noticed the glow of light from the phone and snapped it shut. It might be too far to give Vincent her location, but she was done taking chances. The 911 operator wouldn't care. She'd still send the cops.

A Hummer was parked one car in from the corner. It would make a great hiding place as long as neither Vincent nor Ivan came to start it. She crouched by the driver's door. Losing her line of sight was hard to take, but she was hidden and that was important. And, maybe the fact she hung up on the 911 operator would put a bit of speed into the police. She would give anything to hear the wail of sirens right now.

Footsteps approached the vehicle. Monique held her breath. If Ivan found her now, there would be no way she could stay safe long enough for help to arrive. She fought the urge to run that twitched her legs.

She told herself that he didn't know where she was, or he'd already have her. He wouldn't hesitate. He wouldn't want to take the risk of losing her again. If he found her, she would have to do something she wasn't prepared to do. She didn't have a weapon on her, and nothing was conveniently at hand. But more than that, Ivan was right. She didn't want to become a killer.

A weapon would make her feel safer, though. Why couldn't there be a handy tire iron laying in the gutter?

Why hadn't she kept the chisel?

The footsteps went past her and she carefully turned, trying to be silent. It was Vincent.

Where was Ivan?

Vincent stood on the sidewalk beside the passenger door. Monique leaned closer to the Hummer, her foot shifting a stone. At the sound, she froze. Vincent turned slowly toward her. She felt a tremble start in her gut and take over her body.

If she couldn't hold herself together, he would see her, and she wouldn't be able to do anything about it.

He was looking straight ahead. If he didn't look down, she would be fine.

Monique fought an urge to close her eyes. As much as she didn't want to see him find her, she couldn't afford to be afraid of the truth. It was going to come down to a fight, and he outweighed her, and probably had a thousand fights under his belt.

"Well, did you find her?" Ivan's voice came from behind.

Vincent turned to face his boss. Monique breathed again when his attention was taken away. Where were the cops? If this is how they responded to an emergency, the city was in trouble.

"She can't have gotten far. We'll find her. Do you want me to kill her when I see her?"

"No. We will take her somewhere we can hide the body. Somewhere you can clean up when we are done. I think we can forget this evidence she claims to have. I don't think she has anything. Just make sure she's kept quiet."

Ivan walked away. At least Monique heard footsteps retreating and she could still see Vincent's head. She didn't care that Ivan would get away. She had enough evidence against him for kidnapping to get the police to arrest him, and she had a good idea where they could find him.

Vincent was another matter.

She didn't think he would give up looking for her. She couldn't hide forever. Her legs were protesting being crouched in the cold after the time in the room. If he would just go back, or turn the corner, she could move.

Finally, in the distance, she heard sirens. It was only a matter of moments.

"Hello, did you think you could hide from me?"

Vincent was behind her.

How had she taken her attention off him? She spun to face him, rising from her crouch, feeling the pain of cramped muscles as she did. He reached for her and she dodged at the same time. She felt the pain of her shoulder crashing against the Hummer. She told herself to ignore it. Pain could wait.

"Come here, you stupid woman."

She saw his hand coming toward her and managed to duck at the last second. His hand hit the spinners attached to the hubcaps, and he grunted. Monique rolled to the side while he shook out the pain.

Scrambling to her feet, she tried to run but he grabbed her ankle. The sirens were getting closer, but they would be too late to save her.

She kicked at his hand and heard something snap. He swore and yanked her down to the ground again. Skinning her palms, Monique tried to stop the slide toward what could be her last moments.

"Get her inside." Ivan's voice snapped through the air. "We cannot be here when the police arrive."

Monique squirmed in Vincent's grasp, but he stooped, picked her up, and started for the door. The building was almost a block away.

She opened her mouth to scream. He must have felt her take in a breath, because he covered her mouth. No amount of kicking was going to get her free.

The sirens sounded so close; they could be only a block away. Monique needed to find the energy to slow Vincent down enough to keep the three of them on the street until the cops could see them.

Ivan was determined to get her inside.

She knew he had given up on her handing over the photo. She was going to die, and she could only hope that it would be quick.

Monique did the only thing she could think of, she bit down on Vincent's fingers.

He dropped his hand and stood her in front of him against the wall of the building. She was only steps away from being hidden from the cops. Monique tried to pull herself free as Vincent raised his hand.

Monique only had one way to stop it. "Wait. Do you know who Ivan is?" The words didn't stop him. He slapped her sending bright dots of light through her vision.

"I know who he is."

Through the pain, she saw his hand coming to pick her up again. "No, I don't think you do. He is Javor Dragic, do you know who that is?" Monique pulled away as the lights of the cruisers turned the corner.

Vincent stayed his hand, staring at her with disbelief blooming on his face. Then he turned to look at Ivan who was holding the door open and watching over his shoulder, obviously measuring the risk of being caught.

"Look at him, Vincent. You know what Dragic looks like, don't you? Look at his eyes. He even kept his nickname, The Colonel." She braced herself to run into the street.

Ivan stepped into the corridor as the cruisers came to a halt.

Things started to happen too quickly for Monique to control.

Vincent pushed her out of his way and ran toward Ivan. She couldn't tell if it was to protect him, or attack. Ivan reached around the door with a gun in his hand.

He shot in her direction. Monique felt the spray of brick splinters pepper her face as the shot went wide.

Cops boiled out of the cruisers yelling for everyone to freeze.

Vincent kept moving toward Ivan, his hands reaching out.

Ivan tried to slip behind the door, but Vincent got there before he could close it.

Monique rolled to the ground and curled up against the side of the building. This time she would let the cops deal with the situation.

"I said, freeze," one of the cops shouted.

Monique wanted to close her eyes but couldn't let the scene unfold without witnessing it.

Vincent had his hand around Ivan's throat.

Ivan held the gun between them.

The cops were yelling.

She heard a shot.

Then everything went quiet.

She watched as Vincent crumpled at the knees, his arms around Ivan. She didn't know if he was trying to hold Ivan up, or if he was dragging Ivan down. One of them was mortally wounded.

A cop radioed for an ambulance.

Then someone was standing beside her. "Are you hurt?"

She uncurled and rubbed at the dirt on her sleeves. "Nothing that won't heal."

"Are you the one who called us?"

"Yes. Those two guys kidnapped me and were threatening to kill me. One of them is a Serbian war criminal. The other one killed at least three people. Detectives Adams and Watson know about the murders."

"We'll get you checked out at the hospital and then we'll see about the other stuff."

Monique looked over her shoulder at the two men lying on the ground. "Are they alive?"

"Barely. Don't worry you're safe. What's your name?"

Monique answered questions until the two ambulances arrived. She watched as Ivan was lifted onto a stretcher, a lot of blood staining the sheet they draped over his stomach.

Vincent was face down on the wet sidewalk, his hands behind him in metal cuffs.

21

The next morning, Monique felt every scrape and strain of the previous days. Ivan was in critical condition. Vincent was in jail. She was finished with the police, forever, she hoped. The doctor in the ER had given her some painkillers. Two pills and a hot bath had soothed her muscles enough to let her sleep in her own bed.

Today she'd visit Rafe. Maybe it was time to talk about their future. The idea of looking forward to that discussion was odd, but the idea of wanting a future with someone was even odder to Monique.

She needed to call Tess and tell her she wasn't coming in for few days, her voice felt as damaged as the rest of her. Monique looked for her phone, but it wasn't on the night table.

She was starving so she stumbled to the kitchen before remembering she'd taken all of the groceries to Rafe's the day before. It seemed like forever since she had walked into his apartment to see the blood and damage. A shower and breakfast at Mitch's were her new priorities.

The warm water helped to relax some of the strained muscles and being clean felt like better medicine than the pills.

She dried her hair and pulled on jeans and a tee shirt so she could leave. Monique decided she would start making her calls when she had coffee and pancakes in front of her. Grabbing her phone from the counter, she stuffed it and her wallet into her jacket pocket and headed out.

Halfway to Mitch's, her phone rang. When she looked at the display, it showed Andy's number. It would be Didi. At least she hoped it would.

"Hi, Nique. What are you up to?"

"Breakfast. Are you out of the hospital?" She hurried her pace.

"Yeah, I'm at Andy's. I guess he told you about us." Didi's tone was whiny and Monique wondered what he really wanted.

"Yeah, I guess I'm happy for you. Why didn't you tell me?" She didn't understand the annoyance that started to build in her system. Didi wasn't the problem. In fact, today no one should be the problem.

"I didn't want you to judge. I was messed up on drugs and Andy was helping me. I thought you would be mad that I needed his help."

Just like Didi, reading his emotions into her behavior. Had it always been this way? Had he been afraid of her judgment?

"Didi, I wanted you to get well. I don't care if someone else helped you. I'll be here for you now that you are ready to get completely clean."

"I think Andy can do all the supporting I need, Nique. I don't want to put you out."

Her temper soared. This was just like Didi, making her feel guilty even when she tried to help. Andy was right. He needed to grow up and she wasn't helping. She needed to fix herself before she took on any more of Didi's problems. "Didi, stop being an asshole. I never walked away from you. I always put everything aside for you when you needed me. I have put up with your addiction all these years and never asked you for anything. Why don't you give me a call when you grow up?" Monique clicked the phone shut. She felt a mixture of relief and regret in her heart. Knowing she was doing the right thing for her brother didn't help her feel good about it. It made her wonder if this what it felt like when you let yourself feel something. Was it all anger?

Monique found a table in the back of the restaurant, one that was beginning to feel like her table. Jack put a coffee in front of her before she could ask and took her breakfast order with a smile, but none of the usual banter. Was that her fault? Did she look pissed off?

She blew out a breath and stirred sugar into the mug. She couldn't spend the rest of her life lashing out. She'd call Didi later and try to make peace. Try to meet him and Andy for coffee and find a balance in that relationship.

A stack of pancakes slathered in syrup helped to soak up the remaining irritation. Monique phoned Tess when she couldn't stuff another bite in her mouth.

"Can you get Maisie or someone to cover for a few nights?"

"Monique, you haven't had more than a day off in the last two years. Why don't you just take a week like a normal person?"

Rest sounded great, but she knew that she would be spending most of the time working out her relationship with Didi, and maybe doing the same thing with Rafe. "A week sounds about right. Are you sure?" She felt a little niggle of doubt, was Tess trying to ease her out?

"A week is as much as I'm sure about. You're my biggest draw. I don't want you going anywhere else. You need anything?"

"No, a week is fine. I'll drop by for a drink in a couple of days to see how the new girls are doing."

Tess said she'd hold Monique to that promise and then hung up.

Monique slid the phone into her pocket. Finishing her coffee, she tossed enough for the bill and a tip on the table, making sure Jack saw the money. She started walking to the hospital. Tess's question ran through her mind. Did she need anything?

Maybe it was time to go back to therapy.

Tess wasn't the hard businesswoman Monique thought she was. Could she be wrong about other people? Could she be so screwed up that she couldn't imagine people were able to be kind as well as something else?

FIFTEEN MINUTES LATER, Monique put her head around the curtain that enclosed Rafe's hospital bed. He was laying there with his eyes closed.

He had been beaten badly. His left eye was swollen, and his lips were cracked. Under the blanket, his right arm looked too thick. It must be in a cast. That was going to be a problem for him in his line of work. A keyboard needed two working hands.

Another cast covered his leg.

Maybe if he couldn't work, he'd take some time off too. Monique smiled at the thought of what it took for either of them to take a break.

His right eye opened. "Monique? You're okay." The relief came through the pain on his face. "Those guys are really dangerous. I thought you were dead."

She touched his good hand under the blanket. "Nearly, but the cops came at the last minute. I'm a bit sore and bruised, but you..."

"I'll be fine now that I know you're okay. Is it over?"

She pulled up a stool that was tucked into the corner by the head of his bed. "I guess no one brought you up to date. Sorry about that."

"Not your fault. I've been out of it for most of the night anyway."

Monique placed a kiss on Rafe's forehead to hide her sudden tears. She wiped her eyes before sitting on the stool. "The guy who killed Snake, and those two other guys across the hall, is behind bars along with his boss. He's not happy to find out that he's been working with a war criminal all this time. I'm hoping he'll turn on the guy and let me off the hook for testifying."

Rafe gave her hand a squeeze. "So it's over."

Monique swallowed to loosen her throat. "He said my dad was his role model."

"What the hell. He said he knew your father? That he was a..."

Monique nodded. "Well not exactly, but my dad changed his name. Do you think it could be true?"

"We can find out," Rafe said. "I can find out."

Monique felt the heat of tears on her cheeks. Did she want to know? Would it change anything? "No, leave it. I think it's better left in the past. Maybe I can start remembering the dad I had before he killed my mother."

"That sounds like a good idea." Rafe looked at the curtain around the bed across the room. "So, I guess you'll be moving back into your place? That is, if you ever moved out."

Monique's heart squeezed. Was he giving her an out, or hoping she'd give him one? Being beaten up so badly could have changed his mind about wanting her to live with him, or even to be with her.

"I kind of half moved in. I had my stuff with me when I got to your place. You were gone. But your place isn't livable right now. You can stay at my apartment until the cops are finished with it."

He turned his head to look at her again. "I know you want us to be independent, but could you try living with me? At least for a while?"

She blew out a breath. "I don't know if I can be who you want me to be. I do know something has changed in the last week." She shook her head. "Oh my god, has it been only a week."

He reached for her hand. "You only have to be you, Monique. I was just mad when I said those things. I know you can't let people close. I'll settle."

Tears welled and she bit her lip to stop the sob. When she had control of her throat, she said, "You shouldn't have to settle. I think I can try to embrace the dragons. I'm just going to need a lot of help."

WANT MORE?

International crimes, dark histories, and corrupt lawyers, check out the next City Crime book set in Prague, In The Shadow of The Past. Use the QR code.

Sneak peek on the next page.

If you enjoyed reading The Dragon at the Edge of the Map, please consider helping other readers to find the story by leaving a review.

CHAPTER 1

It was my first vacation in something like five years. At least that's what people back at the office thought. For me it wasn't just a fun trip to Prague. I'd made some shady decisions in my work, but the last one scared me. At thirty-five, I thought I knew myself. It came as a huge surprise to find I was capable of that much violence.

So, here I sat, looking for a way out. A new life. If no one at home found out how far past my personal lines I went, then I had time, but I couldn't count on the secret staying quiet for long.

For this week I had two priorities. One, to find a place where I could start again with a new identity, in a country house that I could rent out for retreats or whatever. A place I could hide away like a hermit for a while. The other priority was money. Living cost less here, part of why I chose the Czech Republic, and because my grandmother came from here. My dad named me Sharka after her. I looked almost exactly like her in the few pictures she had kept from her youth. I thought it time someone from the family came back.

When the seat belt sign pinged off after landing, everyone

but me rushed to turn on their phones and check in with the world. I treasured the last few minutes of peace and disconnection. But now I needed something to do other than stare out at the passing view of buildings and the barriers between the highway and the surrounding scenery. As soon as the phone found a network, it chimed with a message to remind me my roaming plan was active and then welcomed me to the local network. I planned to take advantage of the fact I had a generous data plan thanks to the law firm where I worked as an investigator. My phone, their plan, a great deal and all the privacy I needed — until I ditched my past life permanently.

I had a list of missed calls from Jack Hennessy, one of the partners at the firm. Had my luck failed already? I ignored the notifications. If they'd found out and called the cops, then I would just enjoy my time and face the consequences when I got dragged back. I hated the job anyway, so if they fired me, I wouldn't mind so much. If the police came after me in Prague, a charge of grievous bodily harm would seriously delay my plans. And with the right pressure, someone would call the locals. Jack exerted pressure all day, expertly and liberally.

I turned my phone off and closed my eyes. Jet lag was hitting hard. On top of the nine-hour difference, the last time my head hit a pillow was thirty hours ago thanks to last minute details on a few cases.

The taxi pulled up to my hotel. Just a few blocks from the tourist points but still in a quiet area. Small shops and a couple of restaurants populated both sides of the narrow street. It was warm in the afternoon sun, and quiet. I might get comfortable with the lack of honking and yelling.

The driver took my bags to the lobby and I paid him and gave him a tip. Checking in was quick; I guess they were used to tired visitors looking forward to their bed and a long nap.

· · ·

OF COURSE, now that I could lay on a bed, my brain craved some entertainment. Between jet lag and now a little guilt at not returning a call that might or might not be the precursor to a jail sentence, I couldn't rest. I'd unpacked, and even ironed the few items that needed it. The busy work made me realize how little I had prepared for leaving everything behind. Amassing a load of clothes was never my style, but I should have paid for a second case. My plan hadn't been in the forefront of my thoughts when I packed for a vacation, not an escape. I had a lot of shopping in my future.

The room was small with no balcony, so I couldn't burn off the restlessness by pacing. Even with the time difference, dinner wouldn't be in the next hour. But I was in a new city and possibly my new home. It would do me some good to go out and find my way around.

I grabbed my jacket and phone; the jeans and tee-shirt I wore on the plane would be fine for a stroll. I had an app that would give me a route to walk, maybe end with an early dinner and then I could sleep. It didn't feel like a vacation yet. Exhaustion kind of disconnected me from everything. I hoped that would change tomorrow because I didn't have the time to lay around recovering.

My phone rang: Jack.

I went cold. Why was he so intent on talking to me? To tell me I was fired and dodging an arrest warrant? His hands weren't clean in the situation that sent me on the run. The thought didn't give me much reassurance since he was a lawyer and I couldn't recognize a tort from a contract dispute. I tapped to ignore. I'm a coward.

It rang again. This time I accepted the call because I couldn't count on him to give up. And if I had to face the consequences, I needed to know now. "I'm on vacation."

"It's too early in the morning for me to argue," Jack said in his court voice.

I felt my body go off fight or flight. When he used the court voice, it meant he was going to persuade me to do something. Hopefully he had no plans to ask me to turn myself in or keep me around until the cops came. I tensed again.

"Fine, what is it?"

"I need your help," he said.

Just like the last time, and would I be in worse trouble after? "I'm not in Vancouver."

"I'm aware. I need help in Prague."

I didn't believe in coincidences. No one knew where I'd gone, only that I was on vacation. Jack thought he could put me on a short rein, but I would find out who told him where I was and cut that particular leash. "So, what does that have to do with me?"

"Don't try to lie. I found you there and I can find you again if you move on," he said. "I have friends who can locate any information I want. And will do what I ask without arguing."

I don't know if he meant it to be menacing, but it kind of came off as braggy. "Then they can help you," I said. "I haven't taken any time off in years, Jack." I hoped the whine in my voice didn't sound quite so pathetic in his ears.

"It won't take long. It's not something I can get just anyone to do. I need someone I can trust."

"Did you need help before you found out I was here?" My exhaustion helped me to sound like the bitch I felt, something I usually kept under control. If I'd gone to Hawaii, would he have needed help there? Now that I asked myself that, I realized the answer was yes. Jack had global interests, and some of them were a little shady, and I guessed some of them were more than a little. I could keep arguing or I could get it over with. Knowing what he wanted might help me turn him down. "What do you want?"

"Just listen," he said.

I couldn't believe he spoke to me like an employee. I had never been an employee, always a consultant, and we'd both insisted on keeping our relationship clear. But if I didn't let him get to the point, he would never let me say no and carry on with my holiday. I sat on the bed, careful not to lay down and give in to the inevitable drag of sleeplessness. "Go ahead."

Jack didn't speak for a moment. I heard him cough, as though trying to control his emotions. That got my attention more than any comment about my abilities. Jack didn't show emotion.

"My daughter, Rio. You met her once."

He expected a response and I was in no mood to linger over the conversation. What good would a power move like that do?

"I remember her." Whatever it took to keep him talking and no more. I did recall meeting her though, at a firm celebration. She'd been a very precocious fourteen. The way she pretended to know everything annoyed the hell out of me — until I found out she was about to enter university. Amazing how knowing she did know everything made her less annoying and far more interesting.

"She went to university in Prague," he said. "A private institution. Data analysis of some sort. I wanted her to stay home, go to UBC."

Another pause. But this time I had nothing to say. My brain wondered why he sent a fourteen-year-old to a foreign country. And then it caught up and I realized Rio would be almost seventeen by now.

He cleared his throat again. "She's been kidnapped."

CHAPTER 2

That made me sit up. I'd expected some trouble; a run-in with the cops, maybe a little too much underage partying; maybe a favor to pay her bail. But it made no sense now that I thought it through. Jack had plenty of legal contacts all over the world. He didn't need me for simple things like bail.

No matter how intelligent she was, kidnapped teenagers needed help. She was barely seventeen, and she must be terrified. I might want to say no to Jack because he was a bully and an ass, but I had better reasons. I was not the right person to do this. Rio needed an expert and I lacked that, even at home. "I don't have any connections here."

"You can find connections. You're good at using people. You always have been. That's one of the reasons why you're so valuable to the firm. Did you have all your connections when you started?"

Probably not ones valuable enough to his firm to make up for what I did, but it seemed they hadn't found out yet. "It took a long time for me to find people I could trust. We don't have years." I tried another tack. "Tell me what happened?"

"I got a call. They want money. She's still alive."

"Is that all?"

"It's the core of the call."

"You should go to the police," I said. Avoiding the authorities in these situations might be a knee-jerk reaction. Their success rate couldn't be all that high when it came to kidnappings on a different continent. Too many links in the chain meant too many opportunities to screw up. I still had to try. "They'll reach out to Interpol, it's the best way to deal with this."

"I want you to do this," Jack said. "Keep it quiet and bring her back. The cops won't be able to do what you do."

The silence felt heavy and I started to doubt I got away with the last case. But it was still silence. I refused to give him the satisfaction of voicing my fear.

"You know what I can do at home, where I'm surrounded by my contacts," I said. "You know I can get results in Vancouver, maybe not how, but you've never been interested in the details."

"I have ways of getting details. You can't be naive enough to think I relied on your reports."

"Not naive. It's my business what lines I cross."

"Not just your business. If you commit a crime for information on a case, the law firm is liable."

My heart beat faster. He knew. Jack would never come out and say it, but he knew.

"It could be true, even if I free Rio. If I have to break the law, you won't be able to get them convicted."

"You worry about getting her free. I'm not concerned about prison sentences."

"I haven't said yes," I pointed out. "If I did agree to help, I'm in a different country, a different culture, and I'm not sure I can get in deep enough fast enough to save her."

"Will you try?"

"I don't think you want me to try, Jack. Trying is more likely to get her killed than rescued."

There was silence on the line. This time it had a different feel. It felt like he was making a decision. I couldn't say what made me think it, maybe I just hoped he was, because the only other option I could think of involved a short future for my dreams.

"I can't go to the cops because... There may be some things I don't want them looking at." The confession rattled out as though he was fighting every word. Jack didn't like projecting weakness, even when it came to family.

"You'd protect your shady business at the risk of your daughter's life?" I couldn't believe he would do that. I'm not saying he was a moral guy, but he must know the facts would eventually come out. His reputation in court wouldn't survive.

"Not just *my* shady dealings," he said.

So, he does know.

"I'll take my chances with the police." I controlled my gut reaction to fight him.

He laughed, a mean little sound. "I know you're bluffing. Let's get to the real point. I'll pay you whatever you ask. I'll keep your secret. I made sure no one else knows, so you can trust me."

I let him think it over. Maybe if I kept silent, he'd say something I could actually believe.

He filled the silence. "I'll give you whatever help you need." He was finally starting to sound like a dad desperate to save his daughter.

"If you want Rio back, you want the best people looking for her. I can't believe that *I* am the best you can find." I got to my feet and started pacing; three steps forward, turn, three steps the other direction.

"In this situation, you are," he said. "I won't take your secret to the police if you don't agree. The people I tell will do you more damage than a prison term."

I didn't want to answer him. I knew what he meant, and I didn't know how to keep my fear hidden. Before this I had plans. Being here or being somewhere in Europe. Doing something different. I took a quiet breath and asked, "What's worse than prison?" I knew fear made people assume the worst and maybe I was wrong. If his threat was going to work, I needed him to say it.

"I'll spread the news to the family of the man Hopper killed." Hopper was the client I crossed the line for. All so he could dodge a murder charge. I guess now it was going all the way and helping someone get away with murder.

"So, he wasn't innocent after all." I tried to stall until I could think of another way to save Rio.

What Jack was threatening would send some brutal people after me. People who wouldn't stop looking until they found me, no matter how much I changed my life. No matter how far I moved to avoid detection. "You know what reporting me will mean," I said. "With the cops. I might get away with reasonable force. I mean, I'm just a woman and he's a big man with a violent history."

"A big man, with a violent history, and lots of friends exactly like him."

I still refused to believe he could convince me to help him. I believed I was the last person who would find Rio alive. And I didn't really believe Jack would do that, set a gang after me. He was elbow deep in this too. He had to know I would tell them about his part in everything that happened. He'd be punished and maybe worse than me.

"So, what's your answer? You're going to do this. The longer you delay, the worse it gets for Rio."

Chills crossed my neck at his words. He sounded more like one of the kidnappers than a concerned parent. I could only think of one other tactic Jack might consider.

If you want to know more, use the QR code to check out IN THE SHADOW OF THE PAST.

FREE EBOOK

Claim your copy of Buying Into Death when you sign up for my newsletter and follow Charity as she solves her fastest case yet!

ALSO BY P A WILSON

For more books by P A Wilson

Use the QR code below or go to pawilson.ca

ABOUT THE AUTHOR

Perry Wilson is a Canadian author based in Vancouver, BC who has big ideas and an itch to tell stories. Having spent some time on university, a career, and life in general, she returned to writing in 2008 and hasn't looked back since (well, maybe a little, but only while parallel parking).

She is a member of the Vancouver Writers Social Group, The Royal City Literary Arts Society, and The Surrey Writing Workshop. Perry has self-published several novels. She writes the Madeline Journeys, a fantasy series about a high-powered lawyer who finds herself trapped in a magical world, the Quinn Larson Quests, which follows the adventures of a wizard named Quinn who must contend with volatile fae in the heart of Vancouver, and the Charity Deacon Investigations, a mystery thriller series about a private eye who tends to fall into serious trouble with her cases, and The Riverton Romances, a series based in a small town in Oregon, one of her favorite states. Her stand-alone novels are Breaking the Bonds, Closing the Circle, and The Dragon at The Edge of The Map.

For more information
www.pawilson.ca
pawilson@pawilson.ca

ACKNOWLEDGMENTS

People think that the process of writing is solitary. That's not the case for me. I have help from so many people it would be hard to acknowledge everyone, but I'll give it a try.

The support and inspiration I get from my writer's groups is incalculable. The Vancouver Writers Social Group opens my mind to other ways of telling a story. The Royal City Literary Arts Society gives me the opportunity to meet and share with other writers who have more knowledge than I do. The Other 11 Months group is where I learn about getting the words on the page. And my critique group who helps me find the best parts of the story I want to tell. Thanks to all of the members of these great groups.

Last of all, but definitely a huge part of the process, my beta readers. These are the people who love stories and are willing, and more than able, to tell me if my finished story is ready for you, my readers.